PARENTING ON PURPOSE

Creating a Standard for Your Family

Jamie Dewald

ISBN: 1542746760
ISBN 13: 9781542746762

This book is dedicated to the following...

My Lord and Savior, Jesus Christ—Thank you for your grace and mercy on my life.
My wife, Liza—Thank you for loving me and being my best friend.
My sons, Micah and Jonah—Thank you for giving me purpose and meaning.
My mother, Connie—Thank you for showing me how to love the Word of God.
My father, Chuck—I'm so proud of you for making Jesus the Lord of your life.

FOREWORD

Just a few days ago I sat with all of our staff at First Baptist Concord in our weekly time of staff worship. I was absolutely on the edge of my seat as an incredible young leader, husband, father, and friend bared his heart to us. Jamie Dewald was our speaker that day and he encouraged us, challenged us, made us laugh and made us cry. And then he left us better. Better people and better servant leaders.

That's also all the things that any great writer should do. And that's exactly what this book does! Jamie will take you not into a boring list of things you should do as a parent, but into a story. A real life story. A story that will inspire you but also equip you to be better parents.

For instance have you really thought through what your family name means to your children? In our home there is an Avant family covenant on the wall. From the time our children were very young we emphasized that our name means something. It means something to God. It should mean something to us. But I've never seen an author deal with this quite the way Jamie does. It will be a powerful help to your family.

And have you really been clear about what you want your children to become? Not what you want them to achieve but who they will be? Jamie creatively lays out 14 things that you want your children to become. It will be a rich part of your parenting journey.

We do a lot of things on purpose don't we? We practice to carve a few strokes off our golf score. We set goals to achieve what matters to us at work. We even step on the scales every now and then to see if we are meeting our weight goal. Doesn't it make sense to do the most important thing in our life-parenting-on purpose? Jamie Dewald, in this wonderful book will help you with just that. And we can raise children on purpose who will follow Jesus and make a difference in this world.

Dr. John Avant
Senior Pastor
First Baptist Concord
Knoxville, TN

INTRODUCTION

After serving in student ministry for over fifteen years, one of the greatest lessons I've learned from working with hundreds of families is that our goal as Christian parents is not to raise great kids but to raise great young adults. This book is simply a guide, a tool to help Christian parents think beyond the present. My desire is to challenge everyone who has kids or grandkids to consider what it means to *parent on purpose.*

What if we all were to decide to raise our kids biblically and intentionally? What kind of family legacies would we create and pass down? There is no such thing as a perfect father or mother; nor are there perfect children. We all cling to Paul's words in 1 Corinthians 15:10: *But by the grace of God I am what I am, and his grace to me was not without effect.*

I sincerely pray this book adds value to your family.

Jamie Dewald

CHAPTER ONE

"Hello?" David's voice was raspy as he answered the phone. He looked over at the bedside clock and noticed it was 1:43 a.m. As a student minister, David received many of these late-night calls, which were never good. It usually meant someone was hurt or had passed away. His mind raced back six years ago to when his mother had called in the middle of the night to tell him his father had died.

David quickly came to his senses, cleared his throat, and said with more clarity, "Hello, this is David."

"David, I am so sorry to wake you. This is Hayden Thomas." Hayden was a high school senior in David's student ministry. David had served at the same church and in the same ministry position for more than twelve years. He was in charge of all students starting in sixth grade until they graduated high school. He had seen many of these kids grow up. Some had been born while he was there and were now in his middle school ministry. Others were in elementary school when he met them and had now gone off to college.

David loved his job. In fact, it was his life's calling up to this point. David was now thirty-seven years old, and he still loved being around students. Hayden Thomas was not only one of David's favorite students of all time, but he was a leader in the student ministry. Hayden was the kid everyone wanted to be like. He was popular, handsome, athletic, and a gentleman. But David loved him so much because he was a great young man who lived out his faith. Everyone in David's student ministry respected Hayden. "Hayden, what's wrong? Are you OK? Do I need to come get you?" David had worry in his voice.

His wife Hailey awoke and sat up. She knew the late-night phone call all too well herself. When married to a minister, a wife learns quickly that when tragedy strikes, everyone needs her husband's attention. So instead of being annoyed or alarmed by the phone ringing in the middle of the night, Hailey calmly went into caregiver mode.

"Honey, who is it? What can I do?" Hailey wiped the sleep from her eyes.

"Yes, I am OK, but something bad has happened," Hayden said with a surprisingly calm and mature tone. "Ben Deaton was just in a really bad car wreck. He is alive, but I think he's hurt. I don't know how severe it is, but the ambulance took him to Regional Hospital. I am on my way there now, and I just wanted you to know."

"Do you know what happened?" David asked. "Was anyone with him? Is anyone else hurt?"

"Yes, sir. Do you know Tyler Neal? He has been to church a few times with Ben."

"Yes, I remember Tyler," David quickly replied.

Hayden answered, "Well, Tyler was driving, and Ben was in the car with him. From what I heard, they were on their way home from a party and apparently drove off the road and hit a telephone pole. Tyler got banged up, but I think he is fine. But Ben was unconscious when the ambulance got there. That's really all I know."

"Thank you for calling, Hayden. I am on my way to the hospital," David said in a strong voice. "Be careful, and don't drive too fast." Before David could hang up, Hayden told him one more piece of news. "I understand," David said in disappointment. "I'll see you in a few minutes."

As he hung up the phone and started to dress, Hailey sensed there was more to the story. "What is it?" she asked. "What else did he say?"

"Apparently Ben was drunk," David said, shaking his head. "I'm not shocked, but his parents are going to freak out."

Ben was a pretty good kid but had a reputation for being wild on the weekends. But he almost never missed church on Sunday mornings or youth group on Wednesday nights. His parents were very good friends with David and Hailey. The couples had even gone on trips together. Ben's father was a great man but very naïve as to Ben's reputation. His mother, bless her heart, thought Ben hung the moon. As a student minister, David sometimes heard stories about Ben and his reputation as a partier on Saturdays and church kid on Sundays. In truth Ben really was a good kid, but he cared too much about being cool, fun, and popular. In the past David wrestled with talking to his friends about their child's wild behavior, but he was afraid of what their reaction might be. Would it hurt the friendship? Would they tell David to mind his own business? But now the truth would come out.

As he drove to the hospital, David's heart sank and his mind raced. He prayed for Ben and Tyler, but he also prayed for their parents. He thought about how terrifying it must be as a parent to find out a child was in a car wreck, but he also wondered how Ben's parents would react to their son's being drunk.

The hospital lobby was full by the time David arrived. Most in the waiting area were high school kids, but a few parents were also in the room. David immediately recognized many of the students. Over half were either in his student ministry, or he knew them from being involved on the local high-school campus. Some students were crying. A few were gathered in silent prayer. Overall the mood was somber and the room quiet. Most of the students were huddled around Tyler, to hear his version of the story. Tyler had a few bruises on his face, but otherwise he looked perfectly healthy.

The moment David entered the room, Hayden jumped up, walked over, and gave him a hug. "Any news?" David asked Hayden.

"Nothing yet," he responded. After a moment of small talk, Hayden walked around to introduce some of the teenagers David didn't know. David loved meeting new kids, but he also found it hilarious how many teens responded to him. When they found out he was a student pastor, some automatically sat up straight and used respectful manners.

Others quickly changed the subject from whatever they were discussing or became completely silent. And still more actually ignored him completely, whispering and laughing when he walked away. When David began going to school campuses as a young student minister, these odd reactions bothered him. He didn't understand why some teens treated him so differently just because he was a pastor. But after so many years of ministering on school campuses, he'd learned to laugh it off.

After making the rounds in the lobby, David looked up and saw Jeff Stenson walk in the room. Smiling, he walked over to Jeff and gave him a hug. "Thank you for coming, buddy. You're the best!" David said to his friend.

"Of course," Jeff answered. "I came as soon as I heard." Jeff was one of the small-group leaders for David's student ministry. Ben and Hayden were both in Jeff's group and had been for three years. Jeff was an amazing small-group leader. He opened up his house every Sunday night for the high school boys in his group to hang out, eat, talk, and have Bible study. These small groups were the foundation of David's strategy to build intimate relationships and trust between students and godly adults.

David handpicked Jeff, recruiting him to be a small-group leader, because he was not only a fun guy, but he was full of integrity. Jeff was originally reluctant to accept his offer to be a small-group leader, because he didn't think high school kids would like him. David told him the same thing he told every new small-group leader he recruited: "All you have to do is open up your home, set out some food, and hang out with some great kids. God will do the rest." Now three years later, Jeff was an amazing small-group leader who had grown close with his boys. In fact, he knew them better than David did, which was exactly the small-group strategy David had in mind.

As David and Jeff talked, Ben's parents walked into the waiting room. Everyone stopped conversing and stood. Tyler alone remained seated, his head down in shame. Ben's mother had tears in her eyes as she walked slowly, her head looking up to the sky. Ben's father had his arm around his wife and a stern look on his face. With everyone quiet and listening, they delivered the news.

CHAPTER TWO

"Ben is awake and doing well!" his mother said with a sigh of relief. She brushed the tears from her eyes. "The doctor says he is very lucky and will make a full recovery. He has a concussion, a few broken ribs, and a dislocated shoulder, but nothing internal. He woke up about ten minutes ago, and he was able to speak with us. He is very sore and confused, but besides that, he is the same old Ben." She looked back up to the sky and said, "Thank you, Jesus, for protecting my sweet boy."

The tension and anxiety suddenly left the room as everyone's fears were replaced with relief. Ben was OK. All of the students hugged and smiled. David immediately made his way over to Ben's parents, who were surrounded by teenagers. They saw David coming and seemed anxious to speak with him. Ben's parents thanked the people around them for coming and then walked toward David, who hugged

Ben's mother first and then his father. "Thank you so much for being here," the father said, still firmly embracing David. "We hoped you would be here."

"Of course!" David said as he pulled back. Water now filled his eyes as he shared this difficult moment with his friends. This was the first time since receiving the phone call that David had shown any emotion. He had a unique gift for going straight into pastoral mode whenever tragedy struck. He could compartmentalize his personal feelings and emotions from his responsibility to help people in need. He was a very gifted leader, and he knew the importance of being strong for families who were hurting. But this couple was personal friends with Hailey and him. He was strong for the students in the waiting room, but now he finally showed his pain. His eyes red and watery, he held back the tears from flowing. "I am so thankful Ben is going to be OK," David said. "What a scary night for you both. My heart was hurting for you."

"Yes, that was the worst phone call we've ever received—every parent's worst nightmare." Ben's mother squeezed David's hand. "We are very lucky. God certainly had his mighty hand of protection around Ben and Tyler."

Before David could respond, Ben's father spoke up. "Can we talk in private?" he asked.

David looked around the lobby and saw a room designated for private conversations between doctors and families. He motioned, and they walked together. After they entered the room, Ben's father closed the door behind them. David noticed his friend's demeanor quickly changed as he searched for the right words to say.

"What's on your mind, buddy?" David asked, concerned. Deep down he knew exactly what his friend was going to say.

"This is really embarrassing for me, David, but..." He stopped and then struggled for the right words. "About the accident—"

His wife jumped in and finished his sentence. "Ben had been drinking," she said, a shameful look on her face. "The police officer said he and Tyler were both drunk, which is why they wrecked."

"Drunk! My son—drunk!" Ben's father finally said, frustrated. "Can you believe this, David? I don't even know what to think right now. My head is spinning. I mean, of course I am so thankful he is alive and well, but I just...I mean, I can't—"

"We are just confused," his wife interrupted, "and we wanted to talk to you."

David searched his heart for the right words. From the time he was a young boy, his father had taught him to pray often for wisdom and discernment. "There are many smart people, but few who are wise," his father always said. For years David prayed almost daily for God to fill him with wisdom and discernment just like he did for King Solomon. Especially as a minister, David desired to be led not by his own thoughts and feelings but by God's guidance. He didn't want to be the type of person who spoke first and then thought. When church members sought his advice, David took it very seriously, so he always tried to choose his words very carefully.

But at this very moment, David was torn about what to say. Part of him wanted to say, "I'm so sorry. This is shocking. I can't believe Ben did this." But another part of David wanted to say, "Guys, I love you, but wake up! Ben has been drinking for a long time. He has a bad reputation in school for being a partier, and many of his friends are bad influences on him." But David knew he couldn't say this, even to his good friends. He was not being arrogant or morally superior; rather, he was genuinely concerned for this family whom he loved dearly. He wanted to help, but he didn't know how.

After what seemed like an eternity of inward thinking, David calmly reached out and grabbed them both by the hands. With utmost sincerity, he said, "Guys, I am so sorry. I can't imagine what you must be feeling right now. The most important thing tonight is that Ben is OK. Let's just focus on that. He knows who he is and what he has done. He knows he has embarrassed his family. He knows he is a child of God but has not been living like it. So for right now, why don't we just love on Ben and praise God for his protection?"

Ben's parents stood in complete silence. Neither spoke, but both nodded their heads in agreement. David couldn't tell for sure, but he felt that, inside, they both knew they were partially responsible for their son's behavior.

After a few seconds of silence, David finally asked, "Now what can I do to help?"

"Would you mind speaking with him about it?" Ben's father asked. "Maybe you can talk some sense into him. Maybe he will listen to you."

"I am happy to spend some time with him, but no one is more important to him right now than his own parents. Guys, don't you realize you are the two most important influences in his life? I am happy to help, but he needs you, not me. Don't you agree?"

"Well, I thought we were important to him, but obviously he has been lying to us," Ben's mother said, frustration in her tone. "Maybe he feels he can't trust us for some reason, but I know he trusts and respects you. Perhaps he will listen to you better."

Again David had a check in his spirit. *They don't seem to understand just how valuable they are,* he thought. David stood up from his chair and said with quiet confidence, "Hey, why don't we just stop and pray right now? Let's ask God to guide us all. Let's lift up Ben."

After several minutes of praying, crying, and hugging, the private meeting between parents and student minister was over. "May I go back with you and see him?" David asked.

"Of course," Ben's father agreed. "Ben would love to see you."

After a brief visit with Ben, David drove home from the hospital, his heart sad. He couldn't get the conversation with Ben's parents off his mind. He knew Ben was responsible for his own actions as a high school senior. Ben had chosen to lie to his parents, attend a party he shouldn't have, drink alcohol illegally, and then ride in a car with another drunk teenager—all unwise decisions. But David also remembered what his father always taught him. "Everything comes back to parenting," was a famous phrase his father often told him. Sitting in silence, he began to process these thoughts.

David thought about his father. He missed him so much. His dad had been not only his mentor but, more important, his best male friend. He wondered what his dad would have said to Ben's parents at the hospital. He smiled as he tried to imagine his father sitting in that private room with them. Suddenly a memory came to David's mind. It was the day of his senior prom. He was about to leave the house to go pick up his date when his father pulled him aside. David saw the memory vividly in his mind. His father gave him a hug and handed him a hundred-dollar bill. "Let me take care of tonight, buddy," his father told him, flashing his world-famous smile. "I want you to always remember what I'm about to say."

"Yes, sir," David said respectfully.

"You are a man now, son. And while it is true that you are responsible for your own behavior, I believe that there are two sides to the coin of life. On one side is you and your decisions. And on the other side is your mother and I, and our ability to raise you. Whatever you do, David, or whatever you say or however you choose to live reflects both sides of the coin. We will always be connected in that way. As your parents, our most important job is to prepare you for adulthood. Through our many mistakes, and the grace of God, I believe that we have done that. I trust you, and I love you."

It was now just after 6:00 a.m., and the sun was about to rise. David was fifteen minutes from home and exhausted. But more than just being physically tired from lack of sleep, he was emotionally spent. Recently work had drained him. Student ministry was a fun and rewarding job, but it could also be an emotional roller coaster. One minute a teenager could give his life to Christ and have David on top of world, and the next an unhappy parent might be chewing him out.

After so many years of working in his church, David was certainly accustomed to these ups and downs. By no means was he a mentally weak man—quite the opposite. But the last few weeks were especially difficult, and this night was no exception.

Just two weeks before, David suffered one of the worst moments of his entire ministry. The father of a middle-school kid in his ministry had barged into his office, wanting to talk. David was no stranger to confrontation, but this was unlike anything he had experienced. He was screamed at and cursed out for fifteen minutes. To make matters worse, this father was on staff at his church. This dad was angry and wanted to take it out on someone.

A few weeks before, David launched a learning series on sexual purity for his students. David was well known for taking relevant topics facing teenagers and teaching them from a biblical perspective. During this series, David taught what the Bible said about sexual purity, lust, pornography, and homosexuality. Prior to starting the series, he sent to all parents letters outlining his plans and agenda. He even had a parent meeting to explain exactly what he was going to teach and why it was such an important subject for teenagers. Knowing, however, that some parents might not want their children to attend, he gave plenty of advance warning. David felt it was the wise thing to do.

The sexual purity series was an amazing success. It had record attendance each week, and the response from students was incredible. They were finally starting to get it, and real change was happening. David had never been more proud. And then this father, and fellow staff member, entered his office, and everything changed. The father had recently caught his middle-school son looking online at inappropriate websites, and he was letting David know he held him personally responsible. It was David's fault. The more the father talked, the angrier he became. At one point he screamed so loud that David's administrative assistant came to his door to make sure everything was all right. David told her they were fine and politely asked her to close his office door.

While this father was yelling and blaming David for his son's behavior, David's mind raced. He thought, *Why have you never had any conversations with your thirteen-year-old son about sexual purity? Why do you allow him to have a computer in his bedroom with unfiltered Internet access? As a father, what happens in your house with your children is your responsibility. All we did was to teach the students what God's Word says about sexual purity."*

David knew these comments to this angry father would serve no purpose. The discerning voice inside him said, "He's not ready to look at these points right now. It's not worth it." David just sat and took the punishment.

After the father said everything he had intended, David finally responded. "I am so sorry this happened," he said calmly. "I sincerely apologize for any role I had in this. I hope you forgive me. Before you leave, can we pray for your son?"

The father was speechless. The fight he expected wasn't to be. Instead, David had diffused the situation. After all, this was a good man. He was angry and perhaps misguided on assigning blame, but in his mind he was protecting his son. As the sudden realization came over him of what he had said and done, the father sat silently. All he could do was nod in agreement as David prayed.

Even though David handled the situation well, the encounter wounded David deeply. Many times during his ministry, he had made poor decisions and needed to apologize or be reprimanded. But this was different. All he did was teach the Bible to teenagers who were hungry for truth. It bothered him so much that the father would blame David personally, instead of using his son's behavior as an opportunity to help him understand the power of sexual sin and beauty of God's grace. David wondered what he could have done differently, and how he would have reacted with his own sons.

Another difficult event took place a few days later. It was Sunday morning, right after the church service. David stood in the foyer and talked to families as they were leaving. A husband and wife David didn't recognize approached and asked to talk to him. "Of course," he said. "My name is David. I have seen you guys here many times, but I don't think we have officially met." After some introductions David learned they had attended the church for almost two years. "Do you have kids?" David asked.

"Yes, we have two," they answered. "Melissa is in seventh grade, and Paul is in ninth."

"That's great!" David said, excited. "Where are they? I'd love to meet them."

"Well, that's actually why we want to talk to you," the wife said sheepishly. "They aren't here. They don't like coming to church. We have tried and tried to get them to come, but they just don't want to."

The husband chimed in, as if to take control of the conversation. It was obvious this meeting with David was the wife's idea. "Yeah, but you don't understand," the husband said defensively. "We are a very busy family, and our kids don't stop. They have tons of homework every day. Melissa is on a travel soccer team, and they play every Saturday. Paul plays on a very competitive baseball team, which has, like, five or six games every week. By the time Sunday gets here, they are just exhausted. They like to sleep in and rest, you know?"

David paused a moment, not knowing exactly how to respond or what was expected of him. David hated it when parents constantly used busyness as an excuse to keep their kids from church, so he wasn't going to bite on that one. "It sounds like they are good athletes," David finally said. "What can I do for you? How can I help?"

The wife appreciated the offer to help. "Yes, that's why we're here. We want your opinion. Do you think we should force our kids to come to church? Please don't get me wrong. We both love being here, and we want our kids to come to church. But they never want to come. Stan and I both were raised in church, but we also don't want to push our beliefs on our kids. Do you know what I mean? We want them to find their own way spiritually and not be bitter because we forced them to be here. Does that make sense? What do you think?"

Unfortunately this was a question David had been asked far too many times over the years. Many parents cared more about their children's athletic development than their spiritual development. Or they were more concerned about being their child's friend than being a parent. Although David was appreciative that this couple, and many others over the years, cared enough to seek his opinion, at the same time, the question concerned him because of what it really represented at home.

"Thank you for being honest. I am happy to share my thoughts," David responded with a genuine smile. "May I also ask you both a few questions?"

"Of course," the wife answered without hesitation. The husband didn't respond.

David continued, "When your kids are sick, do you force them to take medicine even if it tastes gross?"

"Yes," the wife slowly answered, not exactly understanding why David asked.

"Of course you do." David laughed, reaching out and putting his hand on the husband's shoulder. "And so do we with our two kids. Our boys can't stand the taste and texture of medicine, but we force them to get it down. Or do you ever make Paul or Melissa go to school, even when they don't want to?"

Feeling confident in her answer, she said, "Oh, yes, education is extremely important to Stan and me. Stan is a doctor, so we've preached to our kids about the importance of school since they were little. There was even a time last year when some mean girls at school were bullying Melissa, and she fought me every day about not wanting to go. But skipping school is not an option in our family. And, like all girls do, they eventually made up and our now best friends again."

"I have definitely experienced the wrath of mean girls in our middle-school ministry," David agreed with a quick smirk. "But the point is that, as parents, we will force our kids to do a lot of things. We force them to eat vegetables, use manners, do chores, go to practice, and so many other things. We make them do the things they sometimes don't want to do, not because we are mean or overbearing but because we love them and know what is best for them. As Christian parents, what is possibly more important than instilling biblical faith in our children. Does that make sense?"

For a brief moment, David thought he had persuaded them. Just maybe his questions and the passion with which he spoke found it's way into their hearts, but he was wrong. "I just don't know where you get off trying to tell us how to raise our kids," the husband finally spoke up. He did not yell, but he was clearly frustrated. "Just because they are busy with school and sports doesn't mean they are bad kids. They just don't like coming to church, that's all. I don't think it's right for you to judge us."

"Sir, I am not judging you at all," David responded in disbelief. "You asked my opinion. I was simply trying to help. I apologize if I have offended you."

"I told Diane this was a bad idea, but she insisted we come talk to you," he concluded. The man walked away without shaking hands or saying goodbye. David stood with a blank stare, his mouth literally wide open, not sure how to respond. After the husband exited the church, his wife turned back to David and simply said, "I'm sorry." Then she followed her husband out the door.

David finally pulled into his driveway at 6:25 a.m. The sun was halfway up, and the sky was filled with several beautiful colors. David loved to watch the sunrise. He turned off the car and sat in his driveway, staring at the incredible sky. He couldn't stop thinking about the recent unpleasant conversations with parents from church. He wasn't angry or bitter, nor was he frustrated *with* them. It was something else. He was concerned *for* them. He felt an overwhelming burden for the parents in his student ministry. "What are you trying to teach me?" he softly whispered, looking into the heavens.

CHAPTER THREE

"I am so excited to get away this weekend!" Hailey reached over and grabbed her husband's hand. "No kids, no sports, no work—just you and me."

David smiled at his wife. One hand was on the steering wheel, and the other held hers. He didn't say anything; he just smiled. David was madly in love with Hailey. Even after fifteen years of marriage and two kids, he loved her more now than ever before. *Marriage is a funny thing, and time certainly changes people,* he realized. When they were younger and new to this adventure called marriage, David loved Hailey in a completely different way than he did now. It wasn't better or worse, just different. He was always attracted to her, as Hailey was a beautiful woman. But now in their late thirties, he was attracted to her for different reasons.

As a man, David never hid the fact that he was a visual being. In fact, his top "love language" from author Gary

Chapman's *The Five Love Languages* was definitely "physical touch," and he enjoyed reminding Hailey of that often. But now at age thirty-seven, he saw her beauty in different ways. He was even attracted to her when she rolled over in bed as she woke in the morning with her hair looking like Medusa's. She would give him a gorgeous smile, stretching her arms in the air. David loved that only he got to see her that way.

But this was only one example of how he loved her uniquely now after so many years together. He was attracted to the way she closed her eyes and worshipped God on Sunday mornings at church. He was attracted to her when she read bedtime stories to the kids at night. He was attracted to the way she walked in the door after working hard all day and the first thing she needed was a hug from him. He was even attracted to how she cried while watching some cheesy romantic comedy. David's wife was not perfect, but she was perfect for him. She was also the perfect example of a Proverbs 31 woman:

> *A wife of noble character who can find?*
> *She is worth far more than rubies.*
> *Her husband has full confidence in her*
> *and lacks nothing of value.*
> *She brings him good, not harm,*
> *all the days of her life.*
> *She sets about her work vigorously;*
> *her arms are strong for her tasks.*
> *She opens her arms to the poor*
> *and extends her hands to the needy.*
> *She is clothed with strength and dignity;*

she can laugh at the days to come.
Her children arise and call her blessed;
her husband also, and he praises her:
Many women do noble things,
but you surpass them all.
Charm is deceptive, and beauty is fleeting;
but a woman who fears the Lord is to be praised.

As great as their marriage was now and had been for many years, this wasn't always the case. The truth was that they struggled through their first few years together. David was working hard to establish himself as a new student pastor at their church, which meant he was out of the house much of the time. Hailey adored their church and loved doing student ministry alongside her husband, but she struggled with sharing him so much with other people. She wanted him home more often. David's greatest strength was also his greatest weakness. He was an amazing communicator when he taught or preached, but he was lousy at communicating daily with his wife. She was always the last to find out anything, if she even found out at all. David did not intend to shut out his wife, but a wedge existed.

The gap in their relationship continued to widen even more. Hailey felt she had no one to talk to, so she shared her frustrations with her mother. David resented her discussing their problems with his mother-in-law, but more significant, he was embarrassed because she was right. Eventually small disagreements turned to big arguments, sometimes for no apparent reason. Many Sundays, David and Hailey put on fake masks to hide their emotions at church. On a couple of occasions, they argued in the car on the way to church and then walked inside together as if nothing had happened. They truly loved each other very much, but their issues were real. Hailey was jealous of her husband's time away from her, and David was guilty of putting his job and ministry before his family.

Over time, the couple learned how to prioritize, how to communicate, and how to say no. They learned each other's love languages and figured out how to meet each other's greatest needs. They valued each other more and more as each year passed. They came to realize the importance of praying for their spouse and the value of being completely honest with each other. They stopped hiding their weaknesses and instead confessed them. They stopped always trying to explain their side of things, and listened more. In time and with work, they changed from being good friends to being best friends, from physical touch to intimacy, and from a good marriage to a great marriage.

"What is it?" Hailey asked. "Why do you keep staring at me?"

"I just love you so much. I'm really looking forward to spending the weekend together," he answered.

David and Hailey were driving from Louisville to Lexington for a parenting conference. David loved attending as many conferences as he could. Any opportunity to learn and grow was his top priority. In the last few years alone, he had attended several amazing conferences on many different areas of life that were important to him. He attended two conferences on leadership, one on financial stewardship, one on spiritual growth for pastors, and one on personal development, and he and Hailey attended one together on marriage. But David had never attended a conference or retreat on parenting.

A church in Lexington, Kentucky, was hosting the parenting conference. Church administrators were bringing in a well-known speaker and author who had written a couple of books on the Christian family. David had read and enjoyed those books, and he was excited to hear this author teach. David was a very gifted teacher and speaker himself, but he was an even better student. He constantly sought to learn from other people who had experienced success in areas of life that were valuable to him.

David and Hailey had signed up for the parenting conference only a few days prior. David heard about it from a friend, who was also attending, and decided to register last minute. The timing was perfect. Their small group had been talking for a few weeks about how much they wanted to discuss the topic of parenting. Then last Sunday night, the group collectively decided they desperately wanted and needed to do a series on parenting, and they wanted David to teach it. Even though David was one of the pastors at the church, their small group consisted of four godly couples, each of which took turns leading and teaching. David loved that he didn't always have to be in charge. In his small group, he could simply be himself. Although ultimately everyone in the group looked to David as the leader, they all did their part and carried their weight, so everyone's gifts and abilities were an asset to the group. But this time they wanted David to teach on biblical parenting. So on Monday morning, when he found out about this Christian parenting conference taking place the following weekend, he immediately signed up and decided to make it a fun weekend with his wife.

"What are you thinking about?" David asked Hailey, after driving a few minutes in silence.

"Actually I was just thinking about our small group and how far everyone has come in the last two years," she answered. "It's crazy, isn't it? Chris and Jess were on the brink of divorce when we met them. Brian and Leslie had just joined our church after that horrible situation in their previous church. And Brian wasn't even a believer but then gave his life to Christ. Do you remember how Scott barely said a word for weeks when they started coming to our small group? Becca had to always talk for them both because he was so shy. It's just amazing how everyone has changed!"

"I do remember," said David. "The most impressive part of it all is how different we all were as individuals when we started, but now how unified we all are. I truly believe I would do just about anything for any of them, and they would for us as well. Even crazier is that I don't think any of us would have ever been friends if not for this small group."

Their small group was extremely important to David and Hailey. They had been meeting weekly with these same three couples for over two years, and everyone had matured so much. David was a big believer in the life-transforming power of an effective small group. He had personally seen so many lives changed, so many marriages restored, and so many new believers mature spiritually because they were involved in a small group at church. In fact, small groups were at the very core of their church's strategy. Every week they promoted to the congregation the same three expectations for personal and spiritual growth. The teaching pastor said these same words every Sunday morning: "We don't want anything *from* you, but we want a lot *for* you. We want you to commit to three things: attend worship regularly, get involved in a small group, and find a place to serve."

It saddened David that most people so easily committed to attending worship and finding a place to serve, but so few got involved in a small group. In David's opinion, real change occurred through involvement with a good small group. Too many families in their church attended the worship service, it seemed, almost out of obligation. They came each Sunday, sat, listened, and then left. But David and the other pastors wanted so much more for their members.

David and Hailey's small group provided a perfect example of genuine life change. From the moment they assembled this group of like-minded believers, David shared his vision to walk and live together in biblical community. He reminded them often that they were all too busy to just have another meeting on the calendar. This small group was about staying connected, doing life together, holding one another accountable, encouraging one another, lifting one another up in prayer, and finally it was about authentic relationships. David often said, "I have hundreds of good surface relationships in my life, but with you guys I am able to go beneath the surface and lay it all out." A few times each year, Hailey read from Acts 2:42–47 and discussed with the group how the first-century church depended on living in biblical community together:

> *They devoted themselves to the apostles' teaching and to*
> *fellowship, to the breaking of bread and to prayer. All the*

believers were together and had everything in common. Every day they continued to meet together. They broke bread in their homes and ate together with glad and sincere hearts, praising God and enjoying the favor of all the people.

CHAPTER FOUR

I t was Saturday night at 5:30 p.m. when David and Hailey walked out of the church. The parenting conference had been over for an hour, but the pair stayed and made small talk with a few other couples they met at the event. Then they got in their car and headed back to Louisville.

"Do you want to rush back home to see the boys or take our time and go out to dinner?" Hailey asked her husband. Whenever David left town or went on a church trip, he always rushed back afterward as fast as he could. He hated to be away from his kids. It was obvious in her tone that Hailey wanted to spend more alone time with her husband. But knowing how eager he usually was to get back home, she wanted him to decide.

"Are you kidding me?" David quickly responded. "Two more hours of peace and quiet and grown-up conversations with you, or loud chaos with the little munchkins? I'll go with option number one."

His answer pleased Hailey very much. She loved her kids more than anything in the world, but she also highly valued adult time with David. In fact, her top love language was quality time, so whenever he suggested they spend some time together, it made her feel special. Hailey was almost always in a good mood. She had a natural joy and energy that was contagious. But now she perked up even more, grabbing her husband's hand, and with a big smile said, "I hoped you would say that. Where should we eat?"

One of the best things about being married to the same person for many years was all the inside jokes. One of David and Hailey's inside jokes was choosing where to eat dinner. When it came to picking a restaurant, Hailey never made the final decision. She loved to talk about it, but when it came down to actually naming the place, she always wanted David to decide. David, being the loving husband, enjoyed messing with his wife. He tried everything to encourage her to make the final decision. One time he even stopped the car in the middle of the road and refused to move until she picked.

"Let's see..." David thought out loud. "We could go to Taco Bell or Chick-fil-A. Or we passed Buffalo Wild Wings on the way here."

"Are you serious, Mr. Cheapskate?" Hailey rolled her eyes. "We have no kids, we're not in a hurry, and I'm dressed up looking pretty. Take this girl someplace nice!" David absolutely loved his wife's playful spirit. He often told her that, as beautiful as she was, he loved her personality and humor even more.

Ten minutes later, they arrived at Buffalo Wild Wings. Pulling into the parking lot, David tried to hold back laughter. Hailey just stared at him with a look that said, "You're unbelievable."

A huge smile on his face, David put up his hand to give her a high five and said, "That's what you get for not making a decision. Come on, it will be romantic." Hailey left him hanging on the high five. David got out of the car first and opened the door for his wife. The couple walked inside, holding hands. All joking aside Hailey didn't care where they ate, as long as they were together.

After ordering their food, they had a great time talking about the kids, their upcoming schedules, and Hailey's job. They loved each other's company and simply talking about life. There was never a dull moment, and rarely was there more than a minute of silence when they were together. She often joked that they would never be one of those couples who hardly spoke to each other while dining out. Hailey loved to talk and tell stories, but she was an even better listener. She wanted to know everything going on with David—not because she was nosy or bossy but because she truly cared about his life. After some small talk, Hailey changed the subject and the tone of the conversation. "Honey, I have a serious question. How are things going at church?"

"What do you mean?" David curiously asked.

"I mean, where is your heart at with student ministry? I know how much you love the teenagers, but lately you don't seem to be your same passionate and energetic self." Hailey said. "Is something on your mind?"

"Oh, I'm fine," David replied, appreciative of his wife's concern. "I love my job—you know that. I truly believe many of the students are getting it. I'm so proud of them."

"Then why do you seem off lately? Please don't hear me wrong. It's nothing you're doing. I just know my husband so well, and I can see it on your face."

"You know me too well," David joked. "To be honest, my heart is burdened recently—not so much for the students but for their parents. A few things happened in the last month that really bothered me. I don't know why, but I can't seem to get over them. I didn't know it was so obvious."

"Honey, it's not obvious to anyone but me," Hailey said, concerned. She reached across the table and took his hand. "I just knew something was going on. You always carry other people's burdens on your shoulders, but I could tell something was eating at you."

"I don't really know what it is. I'm just concerned with a few conversations I've had with some parents. I keep thinking about what I would do if I were in their shoes or what advice my father would have given me in these specific situations. I've been thinking about him a lot lately. I wish I could call him and ask his opinion."

Hailey smiled and gripped David's hand tighter.

David continued. "I've been asking God what he wants me to do. Why has he put this burden on my heart for parents? I spent four years in college and three years in seminary, preparing to be a student minister. I learned a lot about teenagers but nothing about parents. Now I've spent over a decade and a half, teaching and leading students, and suddenly I realize something I've never thought about before. As a church, we provide so much time, people, and resources into equipping children and teenagers, but I think we do a lousy job equipping parents."

"What do you think our church should do?" Hailey asked. "Or what do you think you should do?"

David paused and took a deep breath. He wanted to say so much more, but he held back. Instead he simply answered, "I wish I knew, baby."

"Well, speaking of parenting," Hailey said, "let's talk about this parent conference. I'm dying to get your thoughts."

"Sounds good," David answered. "But you look like you have something to say, so you go first."

Hailey reached over and grabbed her notes from the conference. She skimmed over them, as if looking for something in particular. "Oh, here it is," she began. "Overall I really enjoyed the weekend. Mostly I just loved spending time with you, but I definitely have some thoughts to share. Right here is one thing I loved. When they talked about the importance of praying together as a family and teaching our children how to pray and also how we should pray over them while they sleep, I just loved all of that."

She searched some more through her notes and continued. "Of course we already do some of this, but I felt so convicted that I have not been a prayer warrior for our boys. I pray for them and with them but not really as much as I should. I never lay my hands on them while they sleep and give them over to God. That was probably my biggest takeaway, now that I think about it—just coming to the humbling realization that our kids aren't really *our* kids, that they belong to the Lord. And how...let's see, where is it?"

She read through her notes. "Oh, here it is. My job isn't to protect them *from* the world but to prepare them *for* the world, because they are God's children and he has a purpose and plan for their lives. I just loved that, didn't you?"

"Wow, you said all of that without taking a breath," David joked.

"Ha, ha, very funny," she said.

After his silly joke, David immediately changed his tone. He knew how important it was for Hailey to have intimate conversations like this. "You know, I really enjoyed the weekend as well. Getting away occasionally is good for the soul. Actually I was also convicted that I don't pray for the boys enough. I loved that lady's testimony about how she prayed for her children's future spouses for years, and then all three of her kids married godly people. That was powerful."

"Yes, I actually cried during her story. I thought I saw my tough, strong, manly husband tear up as well," she said playfully.

"No way. My contacts were just bothering me," David replied, with a cute smile that seemed to say, *Busted.* He continued, "The most impactful moment for me was when the pastor taught on Deuteronomy, chapter six. It's funny how you can hear or read something so many times, but then suddenly you learn it anew. There's no telling how many times I've read this chapter, but for some reason it really clicked with me today."

David grabbed his cell phone and pulled up his Bible app. After a minute he was reading from Deuteronomy 6:1–2: *These are the commands, decrees and laws the Lord your God directed me to teach you to observe in the land that you are crossing the Jordan to possess, so that you, your children and their children after them may fear the Lord your God as long as you live.* He paused, looked up from his phone, and stared at his wife. "This is a good legacy." His eyes watered. Hailey was caught off guard by his emotion, because just a few seconds earlier he was joking around with her. He fought back tears. "This is the kind of legacy I want to pass on. This is what my father taught me and what I want to teach the boys. This is what has been on my mind lately. You asked me earlier what I've been thinking about. It's this idea of creating and passing on a godly legacy for generations to come in our family...but not only for our family. I have been burdened for other families in our church."

Hailey wiped tears from her eyes. It was always difficult for her to see her husband cry. "Why haven't you told me about his? Why wouldn't you share this with me?"

"I was afraid," David answered.

Confused, Hailey asked, "Afraid of what?"

"Afraid might be the wrong word." David tried to explain. "I just knew if I talked about it, then I would have to do something about it. I guess I was afraid God was trying to tell me something, trying to tell me to *do* something. I didn't know if I was willing to do it. I believe God has put Christian parents on my heart, and he has given me a specific message to share with them. I have been trying to ignore him." David paused, partly because he was embarrassed by his honest confession but also because he didn't know exactly how to communicate his thoughts.

Hailey slowly grabbed both his hands. With a loving smile, she spoke softly. "Honey, if God has put something on your heart, why on earth would you ignore it?"

"I've been asking myself the same question," David answered vulnerably. "I think it's because I feel so unqualified. Teaching students comes so easily to me, and even preaching to adults is no problem because I'm simply teaching a passage of Scripture. But when it comes to teaching and equipping parents, who am I?"

"David," Hailey said with a sense of pride and confidence, "if God has given you a message for parents, it isn't coming from *you* anyway. It's coming from him. If you weren't humbled by this task, I would question your intentions. Every vessel God chooses to use to deliver his message should start by asking, 'Who am I?'"

David gripped his wife's hands even tighter. He was used to being the giver of advice. He was usually the one who spoke with wisdom and discernment, but this time he was on the receiving end of good counsel. "How did you get to be so wise?" He gave his wife a wink.

"I married a pastor," she answered through her beautiful smile.

CHAPTER FIVE

It was Saturday night, and Hailey had just finished tuck-ing Noah and Joseph into bed. She prayed with them, kissed their little lips, and said good night. As she walked back toward her bedroom, she noticed the light was on in David's office. When she walked in, David was sitting at his desk with papers spread out everywhere. "What are doing?" she asked. "That's the messiest I've ever seen your desk."

David looked up and replied, "It's only messy if you don't understand my organizational methods."

"That makes absolutely no sense at all." She laughed. "But you keep telling yourself that."

"I know I have a problem," David joked. "I think I'm more lost now than when I started."

"Lost about what? What are you studying?"

"We're beginning the topic on parenting tomorrow night at our small group, remember?" David looked back down at his desk and fumbled through his papers. "These are all the notes I've taken over the last two weeks. I'm trying to organize my thoughts and put a game plan together. I know what I want to teach on and what I want to discuss with everyone, but I'm having a hard time putting a structure to it all. It's almost like I have too many notes."

"Well, maybe you do," Hailey offered.

"Maybe I do what?" David was only half-listening.

"Like you said, maybe you have too many notes. Maybe you are trying too hard." She sat down across from his desk.

David stopped what he was doing and looked at her. "There is so much information here. Do you know how much Scripture there is about parenting and raising children...or how many good books are written about Christian parenting...or how many Bible studies and resources I've found online?" David wasn't frustrated, and he wasn't arguing. He was just trying to explain the pressure he felt to provide good lessons for their small group.

"I'm sure there is, honey," Hailey calmly agreed. "You read way more books than I do, and have probably thought about it more than I have. But again I say maybe you are trying too hard. Remember our talk after the parent conference in Lexington? You said you thought it was a great spiritual experience and that you were challenged in some areas as a father."

David listened but didn't answer.

"And then you said you wished more practical information was given. There was some good teaching but not very much to actually apply with our boys. You said Christian parents don't just need theories and concepts but that they need lessons to put into practice with their kids. They want simple, easy-to-understand ways to better raise their children. They desire truth but only if they are able to duplicate it with their families."

All of a sudden, he began to think with a new clarity. He looked down at his messy desk and glanced over his pages of notes. They were filled with good information, but that's all it was—information. He had put together pages of great quotes from famous Christians, articles he had read online, parenting statistics he had found, excerpts from a few of his favorite parenting books, and even the results of some surveys on the importance of family. It was all great stuff, but it wasn't David. He suddenly realized he was trying to be something he was not. He wasn't a parenting expert, so why was he trying to prepare and teach like one?

Although he hadn't said a word, Hailey saw his demeanor change. She watched for a moment as he wrestled with her words. After a moment, she spoke. "David," she said softly, "look at me."

He looked up as if needing her to say something profound.

"You are the best father I know. Just be yourself. Talk about what you learned from your father, and share some of the things God recently placed on your heart. That's it." She paused before adding, "Everyone in the group looks up to you. Just share what you already do when parenting Noah and Joseph. That's what the group needs. And that's what they would appreciate the most."

"You're right," David finally said. "I was definitely trying too hard. Thank you for being honest."

"You know I'm your biggest fan, and I always have your back." She got up to leave.

"I know, baby. I love you." David put the stack of papers down and sat back in his chair.

As she walked out of his office, Hailey turned around and shouted, "By the way, the boys are waiting for you to say good night."

David immediately got up and walked toward the boys' rooms. It was his favorite part of the day.

CHAPTER SIX

O n Sunday night at 6:03 p.m., David, Hailey, and the
boys pulled into the driveway at the Cline residence.
Other cars were parked at the house. This meant the Joneses
and Dentons had already arrived. The Williams family was
last again. They had developed a bit of a reputation for being habitually tardy. Being late was a huge pet peeve for
Hailey, but they seemed to be late to everything. David always joked that he liked to make a grand entrance after the
others had arrived.

Jessica Cline opened the door and exchanged hugs with
Hailey and David. She knelt down and spoke to Noah and
Joseph. "Hey, boys, how are you today?" She hugged their
little necks. Jess was known as the group's hugger, hugging
about everyone she met.

"I'm very blessed. How are you?" Noah responded without hesitation.

A second later, copying his big brother, Joseph stuttered, "Very blessed. How are you?"

"I'm doing great!" Jess replied. "I love your manners."

"Thank you," both boys said at the same time.

"The kids are all downstairs playing, if you want to go on down," she told the boys. Without even saying goodbye to their parents, Noah and Joseph ran downstairs. They loved Sunday nights, because they got to play with the other kids in the group.

"Everyone's in the living room and kitchen," Jess said, motioning to David and Hailey. "What are those papers for? You're not giving us old people homework, are you, David?" Jess pointed to the stack of papers David was holding.

"No homework this week." David grinned.

They entered the living room, where the other couples were already eating snacks and enjoying their conversations. This was Hailey's favorite part of the night. She loved talking to the other ladies and catching up on life. Even though the group met every Sunday night, the ladies talked as if they hadn't seen one another in months. They guys thought it was hilarious. It was as if all four ladies had so much stuff built up inside that they might explode if they didn't get it out. Each week they flocked together and talked a mile a minute about Lord knew what.

Although much less bubbly, David also really enjoyed his time with the other guys. They had gotten pretty close over the last two years. It wasn't just a Bible study group. These men were his friends. He trusted and loved each of them. As usual, the guys sat in the living room, talking about sports, their favorite topic of conversation. Sometimes they discussed politics, news, finances, or something going on at church, but mostly they debated about sports.

"Look who's late again," Brian Denton joked as David sat down.

"I just wanted to block your car in, buddy," David responded quickly.

As the ladies gathered in the kitchen, talking and laughing, the men discussed the latest college football rankings. After about fifteen minutes, Jess announced that it was time to start the small-group meeting. The other ladies followed her into the living room, and everyone sat down. Each week everyone organically took the same seats. Every once in a while, David jokingly tried to sit in someone else's spot.

The group consisted of four families. David and Hailey Williams had organized the group. David, of course, was the student pastor at their church, but he was also the default leader of the group. Actually there wasn't supposed to be any one leader, as each couple was responsible for bringing their own thoughts, opinions, questions, and comments to the group each week. Sometimes they rotated so each couple could prepare a lesson and guide the discussion. But no matter how they did it, David naturally emerged as the leader. He didn't mind as long as everyone brought his or her own gifts, abilities, and experiences to share.

Hailey was a part-time real estate agent. Before the kids were born, she worked full time and made very good money. After Noah was born, she decided to switch to working part time so she could be more involved with her kids. She volunteered often at Noah's school and was the "team mom" for every sport the boys played. David and Hailey made it work financially, and they knew they were blessed. Noah was about to turn six years old in a few weeks, and Joseph had just recently turned four.

Chris and Jessica Cline hosted the group each week at their home. Chris owned a financial planning business, and Jessica, who everyone called Jess, was a personal trainer. They did well financially and loved to open up their home, not only for this small group but also for other ministries. The running joke with the group was, "Who is living in the basement now?" The Clines often took in short-term missionaries or foreign exchange students, and on a couple of occasions they opened their home to single moms who needed temporary support.

They had one fifteen-year-old daughter, who was heavily involved in David's student ministry. Although Chris legally adopted her a year before, the daughter was Jess's child from her first marriage. Chris, too, was married once before. They were both very young, and neither were believers at the time of their first marriages. Both went through ugly divorces and years later met at church. Even though they both gave their lives to Christ shortly before getting married, they had major struggles. Each carried issues and baggage into the marriage, and they almost agreed to divorce. Thankfully as new believers, they tried marriage counseling first. Another pastor at the church counseled with them for months, and ultimately their marriage was saved. Shortly after starting marriage counseling, they joined this small group, which radically changed them. They were both now on fire for Jesus, and their marriage was grounded in God's Word. They even shared their story at church, at the request of the teaching pastor.

The third couple in the small group was Brian and Leslie Denton. Brian was a teacher and head baseball coach at the local high school. Since taking over as head coach six years ago, he completely turned the program around. The year prior, he led his baseball team to win the school's first-ever state championship. Everyone loved Brian. He was full of energy and passion, and he knew how to inspire people. His wife, Leslie, was a pharmacist and a very smart lady. The group often joked, "Since she is so smart, how did she end up marrying Brian?" All of the moms loved having her in the group. It seemed every week someone was asking a medical or pharmaceutical question of Leslie. It was like having a private health consultation for free.

Brian and Leslie had two kids—an eight-year-old son and eleven-year-old daughter. When they first visited the small group, Leslie was a Christian, but Brian was not. They had a pretty good marriage, but Leslie desperately prayed Brian would get saved. They came from a church where Brian had a bad experience, so he was jaded and guarded. But he felt comfortable in their small group, and he really liked David. He and David spent a lot of time together outside of the group, and over time he asked spiritual questions, opened up, and let David in. David led Brian to Christ and later baptized him. The whole small group was at church that Sunday morning of his baptism, cheering Brian on.

The final couple was Scott and Becca Jones. Scott worked as an insurance agent, and Becca was a stay-at-home mom of four. Their kids ranged in age from five to thirteen. The oldest three kids were their biological children, but the five-year-old was adopted. They were a great family, very giving and compassionate. As a homeschooling mom, Becca was unreal. She was so organized, prepared, and planned. The other mothers in the group constantly asked how in the world she made everything look so easy. Scott was the shy one of the group, but he had become so much more outgoing. When the Joneses first attended the group, it was like pulling teeth to get a word out of Scott.

Every once in a while, David joked about it. In the middle of a small-group gathering, David might suddenly shout, "Scott, please be quiet and give others a chance to talk!" Scott was never offended, always laughing at himself. He wasn't rude or unhappy, just shy and quiet. Eventually he opened up and shared his thoughts. The truth was that he probably loved coming to the small group more than anyone.

When everyone finally got situated, Jess spoke up. "All right, you two, I'm excited to hear about that parenting conference you attended."

Hailey took the lead. "The conference was really nice. More than anything, it was great for us to just get away and spend some quality time together. It's hard for us to get away for a weekend, because David always has to be back by early Sunday morning. So it was a special time for us."

Leslie spoke up. "I know exactly how you feel. Once baseball season starts, I can forget about going anywhere with Brian. He is gone every Saturday, so in the off-season, I make him take me somewhere nice without the kids." Leslie slapped her husband on the leg.

"It's definitely important to have time away together without kids and work. I'm not allowed to even mention the word *baseball*," Brian added.

Hailey continued. "The pastor and his wife who led the conference did a really good job. He was a great teacher, and she was precious. They shared a lot of their successes and failures as parents, which was nice to hear. It wasn't all churchy and perfect, you know?"

The other ladies nodded. "What did you learn?" Jess asked, pointing to the stack of papers David had been holding. "Are those your notes or handouts from the conference?"

"No, this is something else we will get to in a minute," David replied. "Although it's funny you ask that, because Hailey and I have been talking for days about that very question. We both enjoyed the weekend, and I am certainly glad we went. Some powerful stories were shared and one really inspiring Bible study from Deuteronomy." David paused, searching for the right words. "Every time I think about what my takeaway was, I have a hard time coming up with much. I'm not being critical at all, but you guys all know me really well. I always say that truth without application is just information, and application without truth is dangerous. My favorite kind of teaching or preaching is when I learn good truth and then can actually apply it to my life. It has to be real and practical. Otherwise most people won't do anything with it."

Brian agreed. "I know exactly what you mean. About three years ago, before we met you guys, Leslie and I went on a marriage retreat with our other church. I told her the same thing. We went through this thick workbook that was provided, and honestly it was good stuff. But I was like, *What do I do with this?* Granted, I wasn't a Christian back then... but still. Even Leslie said it wasn't—"

"Practical," she finished for him.

"Yeah, it wasn't very practical," Brian said.

"You know, that's precisely what we enjoyed about the Dave Ramsey event we attended this summer," Becca said, looking at her husband. "So much of the information was new and overwhelming. Neither of us is great with money, but he did such an amazing job of keeping it simple and easy to understand. We left there with a specific game plan, and we follow his 'Baby Steps' every day now. The proof is in the pudding, because we are seeing real progress."

Scott didn't speak but nodded.

"Hailey and I have been talking a lot about it, and our number-one goal for our time together is not to just go over information or read Scripture, as important as that is," David said. "If we are going to spend the next few weeks talking about biblical parenting, we want it to be practical. We want to all leave here as better parents, don't you agree? So I'm praying everything we discuss from this point forward we can all apply with our children and positively change our families forever. I know that's a lot to expect, but God has put some great things on my heart."

Sensing the gravity of David's statement, Hailey suggested they open up in prayer and invite the Holy Spirit to show up:

"Heavenly Father, we bow before you because you alone are worthy. You alone are holy, Lord. We realize we are nothing without you and can do nothing without your guidance. We invite you, Holy Spirit, to dwell in this place. We ask, Lord Jesus, that you would guide our discussions. I pray for wisdom and discernment for David as he leads us for the coming weeks in this most important topic of biblical parenting. We all desire to be great parents, but we know we can't do it without you, Lord. Please teach us how to raise our kids so they will all fall in love with you and serve you only. Please help us to apply what we learn together. May you be glorified in and through us. Thank you, Jesus, for loving us and forgiving us when we sin against you. It's in his name that we ask these things. Amen."

After Hailey's prayer, the group finished with a collective, "Amen."

CHAPTER SEVEN

"Are you going to finally pass out those papers?" Jess asked. "I'm dying to know what it is."

"Hold your horses," David teased his friend. "That's the third time you've asked. You're like a kid at Christmas."

"You have no idea," Chris chimed in. "You should see her around our anniversary. Trying to keep a secret or gift from her is nearly impossible because she will nag you to death."

Jess laughed and punched her husband in the arm. "OK, OK," she conceded. "I'm just really excited about all of this."

"I am, too," David said, taking over the discussion again. Everyone felt comfortable with asking questions or opening up. This was a small-group leader's dream. But every once in a while, David had to rein the group in if the discussion got too much off topic. "Here's how I want to start," David continued, "and I want to say this up front. There is absolutely nothing special about Hailey and me when it comes to parenting. We make our share of mistakes, and we want to learn so much more. Actually, we're just as excited to learn from you guys as you are from us."

"Absolutely," Hailey agreed.

"One thing I am most thankful for in my life is that I had amazing parents," David stated with pride. "Well, my mother is still alive thankfully, so I still have her. But I also had an incredible father, who passed away several years ago. In fact, yesterday was the six-year anniversary of his death. This day and Father's Day are still very difficult for me."

David paused and looked down at the floor. After a few seconds of silence, he looked back up with tears in his eyes. David was not a very emotional person in public. In the two years this small group had been together, they had never seen him cry or even show signs of sadness. The other members of the group had each cried several times, but David had not. Not that he was afraid to be vulnerable, but he normally kept his emotions in check. He was not embarrassed to cry, but it just rarely happened.

"Before he died…" David tried to keep going, but his voice cracked, so he stopped. He was too choked up to continue. He put his head back down and tried hard to stop the tears from coming. At this point, all the ladies were already crying, and even a couple of the men fought back tears.

Hailey's eyes were also watery, but she remained collected. She rubbed her husband's back. "He has a hard time talking about his father," Hailey said on her husband's behalf. "They were extremely close."

"I'm sorry, guys." David finally wiped his eyes.

The others immediately responded. "Don't be sorry," Leslie insisted.

"I know exactly how you feel," Becca said.

"It's all good, buddy," Brian added. "I'm just glad to know you're not a machine after all. I didn't think you were ever going to crack!" Everyone, including David, laughed out loud as Brian broke the tension. He was always good for some perfectly timed humor or sarcasm.

Hailey picked up where David had left off, after everyone had a good laugh. "Tom was an amazing man, and we miss him very much. Actually both David's parents were truly special people. And don't get me wrong—my parents were wonderful. But when it came to raising us, there was a very real difference between our upbringings. And that's where we want to begin tonight."

Hailey took the stack of papers from David's hands. She stood up and passed one sheet to each person. As she was handing them out, she continued speaking. "My parents raised us in a Christian home, and they loved me and my sister unconditionally. We were a close-knit family, and most of the other kids envied me because my parents were the cool ones in our circle of friends. But there was one major difference in the way I was raised and the way David was raised. He and I have talked about this a lot over the years, but it's still hard for me to explain. Maybe you should do it, honey." Hailey looked at David, waiting for him to take the lead.

"Go ahead, baby," he responded. He had regained his composure, but he wanted Hailey to share. She was normally too eager to let him talk for her. She was an excellent communicator who always spoke from the heart, but she gave herself little credit. David wanted her to talk more, because what she said was always heartfelt and real.

"Well, please chime in if I don't explain it well." She laughed.

"Oh, honey, you will do fine," Jess insisted.

Hailey continued, "Looking back, I think my parents did a good job with the areas that were important to them. They were very focused on our education, and they insisted we get good grades, which we did. And of course we were in church every Sunday morning and Wednesday night. My parents both loved the Lord very much, and I am thankful they taught us to love him also. It was also extremely important to them that we stay out of trouble. They were very strict but not in a bad way." As she spoke, Hailey smiled as memories flooded her mind. "My sister and I were both good girls morally, but I think it's probably because we were too scared of what Dad would do if we messed up." Hailey laughed at her own words, thinking how silly that sounded.

"I think we had the same parents," Leslie said, laughing with her. "I was known as the 'good girl' at my school." She used her fingers to make quote signs in the air. "I mainly just didn't want to get punished by my father, but I guess it worked." She smiled.

"So what was the major difference in how you were raised compared to David?" Scott surprisingly spoke up and asked.

"Right," Hailey said as she got back on point. "My point is, while my mom and dad were both good parents, they were mainly focused on us being good girls, getting good grades, and not doing bad things. As long as we did those things, everyone was happy. But there is much more to parenting than that."

"Exactly," David interjected. "Her parents, who I love dearly, were like the majority of parents I've known over the last decade and a half of student ministry. They are good people, they love God, they love their kids, and they try their best. The difference is that my parents took it one step further, especially my dad. He told me a million times, 'I'm not trying to raise a good boy; I'm trying to raise a good man.' The major difference, Scott, is that my parents were more intentional and strategic in how they raised me, compared to Hailey's parents. They weren't perfect, but they were definitely purposeful in everything they did...and I mean everything had a purpose." David smiled.

"Is that what this is?" Chris held up the paper Hailey had handed out.

"A little bit, I guess, but not really," David half-answered Chris and then looked over at Hailey.

"This is something I wanted everyone to have," Hailey explained. "David wasn't sure about handing these out, but I thought you guys would love this."

"It's not that I didn't want you to have it," David quickly responded. "I'm just not positive it goes along with what I wanted to cover during this parenting topic. But it's still great stuff."

"So what are these twenty-five things?" Jess asked, scanning the list on her handout. "Is this something you guys made up?" Jess leaned up in her seat. "This looks incredible!"

"Would someone please explain what this paper is so Jess will stop asking?" Brian asked sarcastically. Everyone laughed.

"I didn't mean to cause such a frenzy," Hailey said, continuing to laugh at Jess's enthusiasm. "I'll explain what this is and why I want you guys to have it. As David said, his father passed away six years ago. He was diagnosed with cancer right about the same time we got pregnant with Noah. Since he knew he probably wouldn't be around to see Noah or help teach David how to be a good father, he kept a journal during his final months. He wrote down the most important parenting lessons he wanted to leave for David and me. These were lessons he and his wife used in raising David. For each parenting lesson, he also wrote a couple of pages of explanation, details, examples, and personal stories."

"Wow," Becca responded. "That is so amazing!"

"What's even more amazing is how it all came together," Hailey continued. "Tom worked on his journal for months, a little bit each day. He got really sick in the end, but by the grace of God, he finished it the day he died. He wrote his last journal entry literally hours before he passed. He was a special man." Hailey smiled at David and grabbed his hand. "He left this final gift for David before he went on to be with Jesus."

"That is the most beautiful story I've ever heard," Jess replied emotionally. "This is the list he left for you?"

David nodded. "These are the twenty-five parenting lessons Hailey and I have used with our boys every single day for the last six years. We have certainly not perfected them all, but we work on them constantly. As you can see, most are very simple and practical, which is what we love."

"You know, it's funny," Chris said. "Your boys are so well mannered and behaved. As I read through this list, I can see several of these lessons in your kids. I've always wondered what you guys were doing to have such great kids."

"Well, thanks, buddy," David humbly replied. "We have a long way to go with Noah and Joseph, but we are very blessed so far."

"I just want you guys to have a copy of these lessons," Hailey chimed in. "As you can see, all of the words are written in masculine since it was from Tom to David, but it applies to daughters as well. David doesn't want to spend much time on them right now, but these lessons have molded us as parents, and since we are talking about biblical parenting, I thought you would enjoy it."

25 Parenting Lessons
Lesson 1: Fathers Are So Important
Lesson 2: A Biblical Foundation
Lesson 3: I Love Your Mother
Lesson 4: The Journal
Lesson 5: Above All, Teach Self-Discipline
Lesson 6: The Power of Repetition
Lesson 7: The Value of Manners
Lesson 8: I'll Always Do What I Say I'm Going to Do
Lesson 9: Trust and Open Communication
Lesson 10: Please Forgive Me
Lesson 11: Teach Money Lessons
Lesson 12: The Importance of Work Ethic
Lesson 13: The Thankful Bench
Lesson 14: Success Mottoes
Lesson 15: The Forbidden Phrase
Lesson 16: Develop His Leadership Skills
Lesson 17: Promote Health Consciousness
Lesson 18: Remember What's Really Important
Lesson 19: Be Interested in His Interests

Lesson 20: There's No Such Thing as Privacy
Lesson 21: Make Special Times Special
Lesson 22: You Can't Hug Enough
Lesson 23: Teach Him to Think for Himself
Lesson 24: Raise Young Men, Not Old Boys
Lesson 25: Pray Consistently

David had other things he wanted to get to, so he moved the conversation along. "I am honored for you guys to have my dad's list of parenting lessons, but we can move on to what I really want to discuss tonight."

"Hold on there, big boy!" Brian interrupted. "My little brain can only handle so much at once. Aren't we going to talk about these lessons?"

"Hailey wanted you to have this list as a reference, but it's actually not what we have planned for this parenting series. I want to go a bit deeper and in a different direction, if that's OK."

"Yeah, that's fine," Brian agreed. "But this looks like good stuff. Can I ask a question before we move on?"

"Of course," David answered.

"What in the world is 'the forbidden phrase'?" he asked.

"And what did your dad mean by 'raise young men, not old boys'?" Chris asked.

"I would love to hear your thoughts on the lesson about teaching kids how to think for themselves," Scott commented. "That sounds very interesting."

"Have you guys already started teaching your kids about money?" Becca asked. "Like, what do you teach them about money at their age?"

"While everyone else is asking, I guess I should too," Leslie said. "Can you explain 'the thankful bench'? Is that a metaphor, or an actual bench?"

David looked over at Hailey and smiled. "Do you see what you've started? This is your fault." He pointed at her and laughed. David put his notes down. Even though he wanted to move on in a different direction and had much to cover, he knew it wasn't the right time. He was just excited his small group was asking questions about his dad's lessons. The other things God had placed on his heart could wait until next week. David had been in ministry long enough to know that sometimes the Holy Spirit takes events in a different direction than expected. He would just have to set his preplanned notes and agenda to the side to let God lead.

For the next hour, David and Hailey answered questions about the twenty-five parenting lessons. David was shocked at how interested his friends were and how much more they wanted to know. Hailey was not surprised. As time went on, a sense of pride swelled up in David. He didn't say anything about it, but he felt as if his father were alive in these lessons. It was as if his legacy were living on. It was the best small group they had experienced in two years.

After an hour of incredible discussion, the group was finally ready to finish up, pray, and head home. Right before David was about to close in prayer, the normally quiet and reserved analytic of the group spoke up. "Hey, David," Scott said. "Thank you for sharing your father's parenting lessons tonight. This is really great information. You should consider writing a book about it."

CHAPTER EIGHT

"It's about time you guys showed up. I've been wanting to share something exciting with you," Jess Cline said as she opened the door. She invited David, Hailey, and the boys to come in. It was Sunday night, and the Williams family was fashionably late for small group as always.

"Can we at least come in from the cold first before you tell us?" David jested.

Jess laughed. "Yes, come in. I'm sorry. I'm just very anxious to tell you what happened. Let's go in the kitchen, so I can tell everyone at the same time."

They greeted and hugged as they all chatted in the kitchen. The men, normally in the living room and talking about sports, also stood sharing stories with the group in the kitchen.

"OK, you guys aren't going to believe what happened," Jess said, looking at David and Hailey. When the others heard her excitement, their conversations stopped as they all listened to her story. "After last Sunday I felt extremely convicted about that lesson on asking our kids to forgive us. I could hardly sleep, thinking about it. You know when God puts something on your heart and you know you need to do it."

"I definitely know that feeling," Leslie agreed.

"Well, I loved what you guys said about how sometimes we don't just need to apologize to our kids—we need to go a step further and ask them to forgive us," Jess continued. "So I sat Caroline down yesterday and had a long talk with her. She is fifteen, as you know, and she can be sassy at times. I know it's partly my fault for letting her get away with it for years. Chris reminds me all the time." She looked over at her husband as if waiting for him to comment, but he didn't. "Anyway, a couple of weeks ago, when she was being sassy, I snapped back and called her a name I'm not proud of."

"Unfortunately I know that feeling as well," Leslie agreed again.

"I felt terrible about it, and I immediately apologized," Jess said. "But after last Sunday, I realized that, as a Christian, I needed to ask her to forgive me. I sat down with her and told her all about our conversation and everything I learned from it. I even told her I have failed her as a mother in some areas. Then I read that passage you gave us, David, from Matthew 5:23–24. I said, 'Caroline, will you please forgive me for calling you that horrible name?'" Jess cried as she told the story.

"What did Caroline say?" Hailey asked.

"It was amazing, Hailey," Jess answered. "She couldn't believe I was asking her for forgiveness. She not only said yes, but she also cried and asked me to forgive her for how she had been treating me. It was one of the most special times we have ever had together. It was the breakthrough our relationship has needed for a while." Chris smiled and put his arm around his wife in support.

"That is so cool," David said, smiling and giving Jess a hug. "I'm so happy for you and Caroline."

"I want to share an update from last week as well," Becca addressed the group. "Scott and I absolutely loved your idea, David, about the thankful bench that you guys do with your boys. We went home and created our own version. We have a sofa on our back porch, so we designated that as our thankful bench. Tuesday night after dinner, I took each kid out there one at a time and explained what the 'thankful sofa' is and why we are doing it now. Then the kids and I shared what we all are thankful for. It was special."

Even Scott spoke up. "We definitely don't spoil our kids, probably because we can't afford to." He laughed. "But we have not done a great job of teaching them to be grateful and thankful for everything the Lord blesses us with. We are excited about this new tradition."

"It's definitely been a good practice and discipline, not only for our boys but for us as well," David commented. "Get ready, because sometimes they say the funniest things. One time Joseph said he was thankful because Noah got spanked for being mean to him." Everyone laughed hysterically. "Needless to say, I had to remind him of the purpose of the thankful bench."

In her normal fashion, Jess took over. "We only have an hour," she said. "Let's head into the living room and get started."

"Yes, drill sergeant!" David joked.

As they all sat down, Brian spoke up. "This isn't a long story," he said, "but I went out this week and bought two journals for our kids. I have never in my life written a journal entry, but I'm really looking forward to it. I think it will be cool to one day give our kids a journal that documents their childhoods." He looked at David. "Remind me to talk to you later about what kinds of things you write in your journals for the boys."

"You got it, buddy. I'm proud of you." David glanced around and intentionally looked at everyone in the eyes. "I can't tell you guys how excited I am to begin our discussion tonight, but I am also humbled. It's very important to Hailey and me that we don't come across as perfect parents or as if we have somehow figured everything out. Nothing is further from the truth."

Hailey nodded in agreement.

"What we do have," David continued, "is an intense desire to become great parents. We want to discover with you guys what we all can do to raise our kids according to God's Word. As we begin, I want to ask everyone a question. Don't answer yet, but just think about it. Ask yourselves, 'What does it mean to parent on purpose?'" David paused and looked around the room.

"I can already tell this is going to be good tonight!" Jess said in her normally bubbly voice. Everyone laughed, not because of what she said but how she said it. Jess got excited about everything, so the group enjoyed joking with her about it. Everyone loved her personality and the joy with which she lived each day.

"I hope I don't let you down," David said with a smile. "In all seriousness, I want to share what has been heavy on my heart for a while…and what I believe God has placed on my heart to share with you. First let's pray and ask God to show up." He said to Hailey, "Honey, will you pray?"

After Hailey said a beautiful prayer, she turned it back over to her husband.

"A few instances at church lately have really caused me to think a lot about this question: What does it mean to parent on purpose? And to be honest, I feel burdened recently because I realize many parents in our ministry just seem to be going through life merely hoping their kids turn out well. They are not bad people. In fact, they are great people who love their kids more than anything in the world. But when it comes to raising kids, it can be easy to slowly shift into random parenting versus purposeful parenting." David stopped and looked around at the group. From the looks on their faces, he didn't think they were following him yet. "I don't think I am explaining it well. Open your Bible to Deuteronomy, chapter six, and let's read verses four through nine. Does anyone want to read that for us?"

"I got it," Hailey said. She gave everyone a minute to find it before she read.

Hear, O Israel: The Lord our God, the Lord is one. Love the Lord your God with all your heart and with all your soul and with all your strength. These commandments that I give you today are to be on your hearts. Impress them on your children. Talk about them when you sit at home and when you walk along the road, when you lie down and when you get up. Tie them as symbols on your hands and bind them on your foreheads. Write them on the doorframes of your houses and on your gates.

When Hailey finished reading, David look around and asked, "When you hear these purposeful and powerful verses and commandments, what do you think of? What do you notice? And what does this passage have to do with us?" David looked around and waited for someone to answer. Several seconds ticked by in silence, but he didn't mind. He was the king of getting people to open up and talk. One method he used to his advantage was the awkward silence. He thought it was a mistake when small-group leaders asked questions of their group and then answered their own questions. Too many leaders were afraid of silence, but David was not. From his years of experience leading groups and counseling people, he found power in influencing people to talk or answer questions by allowing silence to linger. Some of the most special moments of his career occurred just beyond the dreaded awkward silence.

Finally after what seemed an eternity, which was actually only about thirty seconds, the quiet one spoke up. "I have read this passage many times, but I just noticed something I haven't thought about before," Scott said. He looked down at his Bible and spoke as if piecing together a puzzle while he talked. The group's analytic was figuring something out. "Becca and I have a picture frame with this same passage on our living room wall. We know how important it is to teach our kids about the Bible, but I think somehow I skipped the verse that deals directly with me."

Scott, still looking down at his Bible, read, "*These commandments that I give you today are to be on your hearts.*" He looked up at David and said, "When it says *you*, that means *me*. How can I teach my kids the commands of God if they aren't first on *my* heart?" He emphasized the personal pronouns to make his point clear. "Wow, that's a gut check. If I'm being honest, I must admit I don't spend hardly any time personally in the Word. I make sure our kids do, and we obviously take them to church. As a family we discuss the Bible all the time, but I don't actually read it myself." He stopped talking, but it was clear he was still thinking.

David nodded and grinned as if to say he understood, but he didn't speak. He just looked around and waited for someone else to talk.

"Well it's clear God wants us to teach our kids about him," Jess shared with the group. "I don't think he wants us to literally write Scripture on the walls of our homes, but I do think he stresses the importance of passing our biblical faith on to our children."

Chris chimed in, like he was finishing his wife's thoughts. "If we want our children to live out our Christian faith in their own lives, then as parents we must be intentional about teaching them what the Bible says."

David smiled and said, "Exactly! It's a mistake for parents to simply hope their kids follow Christ. Hope alone doesn't mean anything. We certainly can't make our kids love Jesus, but this passage teaches me that my role as a father is to be purposeful in how I raise them." He looked at Hailey. "Our responsibility is to the spiritual development of our boys. Do we actually have a plan? Are we truly parenting on purpose? Or do we just randomly hope our kids turn out well and end up following Christ? These are questions I want us to answer together during this study."

Everyone in the room was nodding in agreement and smiling. They were completely locked in and ready to learn. They knew David and Hailey didn't have all the answers but that together they could all grow as a group. As stated in Proverbs 27:17, *As iron sharpens iron, so one person sharpens another.*

"OK, I want to switch gears a bit and ask you guys a question," David said. "In your minds I want you to see all of your kids as adults. Pretend they are eighteen years old and ready to take on the world. Here's what I want you to think about. What's important to you for your young adult children? What are the most important things you want for them?"

"That's easy," Chris answered. "I want Caroline to go to a good school. She says she wants to be a doctor. I want her to attend the best college available, instead of her following her friends wherever they go."

When Chris finished, Brian shared. "A good college is definitely important to us as well, but for that to happen Matthew has to get a scholarship. He's a heck of a good baseball player, and I truly think he has what it takes physically and also between the ears to be successful. I guess it's the coach in me speaking, but I can't think of a situation where I would be more proud than if he got a chance to play college ball at a Division One school. He and I are working really hard to make that dream a reality."

The conversation picked up, as everyone enjoyed talking about their kids and imagining how they would turn out. Becca joined the discussion and added, "I want our kids to choose careers they love. I don't want them to end up working at some job they hate. The money they make isn't as important to me, but I definitely want them to choose good careers where they can use their gifts and serve others. If my kids were all eighteen right now, I would encourage them to choose their careers wisely and only do something they love."

Jess, somewhat joking but partly serious, finished up the discussion by saying, "Well, you all know my story about my first marriage at eighteen. I was stupid and married the wrong guy, despite my parents begging me not to. The type of man my daughter marries is important to me. I want her to have only one marriage and for it to be with a wonderful and godly man who respects her. She and I talk about it often. That's definitely the most important thing for me." She paused. "That discussion was so much fun. I loved hearing everyone's answers. What a great question, David!" Everyone laughed at how Jess found the fun in everything.

"I also enjoyed hearing everyone's answers," David replied. "College, sports, career paths, and who our kids choose to marry are also extremely important to Hailey and me."

"Why do I suddenly feel like I gave the wrong answer?" Brian quickly interjected. Everyone roared with laughter, including David.

"No, no, it's not that at all," David assured him. "Everyone's answers were perfect. I just want to issue a challenge during this parenting series. I want us to start thinking differently on some things."

"What do you mean, David?" Jess was curious.

"Well, let me say it this way," David answered. "When our boys one day are young adults, the factors everyone just shared will also be important to us. In fact, they are extremely important. Here's the distinction." David looked around and made eye contact with each person. "All those elements—career, college, marriage, sports—are things we want our children to *do* one day. I want to focus more on who they *become* as adults. Who they become as young adults ultimately determines what they choose to do with their lives." The room went silent. Everyone was in deep thought, so David continued. "I want to share a quote with you. One of my favorite authors is Andy Andrews. Hailey has read some of his books as well."

"Yeah, you guys would love his books," she agreed.

"Andy made a great quote on one of his podcasts that has radically shifted my way of thinking and parenting. He says, 'I'm not interested in raising good kids. I'm interested in raising pretty good kids who turn out to become great adults.' I just love that," David said.

Hailey picked up the conversation. "I have actually learned a lot of this from David as well. I'm one of those people who is so busy with life that sometimes I can only live in the moment. David has taught me to begin with the end in mind. In other words, we should know exactly what outcomes we want to see in our kids and then parent intentionally to achieve those outcomes."

"That makes complete sense," Leslie responded. "I'm the same as you, Hailey. I can't seem to look beyond each day. Sometimes we get so busy with school, homework, sports, work, and church that I don't even think about anything else but surviving."

"Exactly!" David agreed. "You make my point perfectly, Leslie. This is why my heart is burdened for Christian parents and more specifically the notion of what it means to parent on purpose."

"When you say, 'parenting on purpose,' what exactly do you mean?" Scott asked. "I might be wrong, but I feel like everything Becca and I do is on purpose. Can you elaborate?"

Becca interrupted before David could answer. "I don't know if I completely agree with that, dear," she said to her husband. "I would like to think everything we do is on purpose, but half the time I'm just going through the motions of the day. And then a day turns into a week...and then a month. With four kids and homeschooling and church activities, I just don't know." She paused, searching for her words. "Scott, I think that we are intentional about school and other things, but I can't say I have ever really thought about who the kids will become as adults." Scott respectfully nodded in agreement.

David sensed something special was happening, as his friends now thought about these questions for the first time. He knew exactly how they felt because it was the same thing he had been stewing on for months. He didn't want to miss the moment, so he pressed on. "Before we finish up, I want us all to think about two questions tonight and throughout the week before we meet again next Sunday. We don't need to answer these questions right now, but I certainly hope that together we can soon find some solutions. The two questions are—"

"Wait, hold on a second." Jess stopped David as she reached for her pen. When she was ready to take notes, she said, "OK, go ahead."

David grinned. "Now that everyone is ready, the first question is this: What specific qualities, traits, and characteristics do we want to see in our children when they become adults?" He stopped long enough for everyone to write it down. "Second, how do we know if we are doing a good job as parents? In other words, is there a standard by which we are raising our children, or are we simply hoping they turn out well?"

Everyone wrote as fast as they could, trying to get it down word for word. When everyone finished writing, they all looked up at David. He looked over at Hailey and grinned. Without saying a word, he spoke to his wife. *I think this is going to make a real difference for some great families,* he thought. Hailey heard every unspoken word.

David concluded the small group by adding, "Think about these two questions, and come back next week prepared to share and discuss. But let's do more than just think about it. We'll all commit to bathing it in prayer, asking God to reveal to us his wisdom and guidance."

Everyone nodded in affirmation, the atmosphere like a locker room before a big game with its emotional mix of excitement, nervousness, clarity, and confusion.

"Everyone, have a blessed week," David said as he closed. "I love you guys!"

CHAPTER NINE

"Those boys about wore me out!" David said to Hailey, although he could barely speak. He huffed and puffed, sweat was dripping down his face.

"Are you really out of breath from playing football in the backyard? Somebody needs to get in better shape," she poked at her husband.

"Tell me about it," he agreed. "Those boys have boundless energy. They never stop."

It was Saturday afternoon, and the Williams family was enjoying a rare day at home with nothing on the agenda. They loved these days—no school, no sports, no church, no work, and no activities...just laziness and family time. It was very important to David and Hailey to create these moments. They had many friends who allowed work, travel sports, and extra activities dominate their lives in such a way that they had limited time to relax, rest, and recover—not to mention time to be together as a family. They themselves had been wrapped up in this fast-paced lifestyle in years past, but recently decided to make some changes and slow down. They'd had to learn how to say no and how to prioritize what was really important to them.

David plopped down on the sofa across the room from Hailey. "You sure do look good for an old gal." He smiled as he gave her his famous tagline.

"Thanks...I guess," she replied.

"What are you doing over there?" he asked her.

"I was just about to send out a group text about the homework we discussed last week. I want to follow up with everyone."

"Great, there's nothing better than being stuck in a group text," he joked.

Hailey smirked and gave David *the look*.

"Oh, no, I know that look. Actually, that's a good idea, honey. It will be interesting to hear what everyone says." David hopped up and left the room. "I'm going to go take a shower," he shouted.

"Good idea," Hailey replied. She hits the send button after finishing her text.

Hailey: I've been thinking all week about our two questions. Can't wait to hear everyone's thoughts.

Jess: I have a list of qualities. It's short, but it's a start.

Brian: I think I have gone through 20 sheets of paper already. I keep starting over.

Jess: Yeah, it's way harder than I thought too.

Becca: Scott and I have talked about it every day.

Leslie: So have we. Every night before bed.

Jess: I can't wait to hear what you guys came up with.

Hailey: Me too. See everyone tomorrow night.

David: My wife is hot!

Hailey: David, you dork.

Brian: Suck-up.

The next night at small group, everyone arrived on time—even the Williams family. But this time there was very little small talk in the kitchen among the ladies or sports talk in the living room with the guys. Everyone gathered in the living room with Bibles, paper, and pens, ready to start. Becca opened up the group with a beautiful prayer, and then everyone turned to David.

Before he could begin, Jess spoke up. "Oh, I almost forgot. I'll be right back." She jumped up and ran out of the room, returning minutes later with a giant dry-erase board. "Look what I bought." She giggled.

"You're not going to write all my sins on that thing, are you?" Brian asked, trying to be funny.

"Honey, that board isn't big enough for that," Leslie quickly fired back. Everyone bent over with laughter, because Leslie had finally outwitted her husband. Brian was usually the witty, sarcastic one, but this time his wife bested him. Fortunately, he could take it just as well as he could dish it out, so he laughed harder than anyone.

Jess regained everyone's attention and said, "I thought it would be a good idea if we wrote our list on the board for everyone to see—you know, the list of qualities we are creating."

"Great idea," everyone agreed.

"OK, let's pick up where we left off last week," David said. "We have two questions that we are trying to answer together. What are they?"

"I've got them right here," Scott answered as he looked down at his notes. "I'm paraphrasing, but number one, what qualities and traits do we want to see one day in our adult children? And number two, is there a standard by which we are raising our kids?"

"Exactly. Thank you, Scott," David agreed. "Are we just randomly going through the motions and hoping our kids turn out well, or are we truly parenting on purpose? I will explain this more later, but I want to say up front that I believe that the answers to both of these questions are one and the same. In other words, as we create our list of qualities that we want to see in our children when they become adults, then we are by default also creating a standard by which to raise them. Does that make sense?"

"You may have lost me there," Brian admitted.

"It's OK, we'll come back to that later," David said with a smile. "Maybe I didn't explain it well. We'll just get started and see where the night takes us. We all agreed last week that instead of focusing so much of our attention only on what we want our kids to do or achieve, our main passion should be directed on who they can become. In other words, we don't just hope they turn out well as adults but guide them and help shape them into specific kinds of adults. By specific, I mean the exact list of qualities and traits we are going to create now."

Everyone was completely focused. David had such a way with words. He could make something that was difficult or confusing suddenly seem easy. At the same time, he could take something that seemed easy and suddenly make it important. He was not an academic or a scholar, but he was good at explaining concepts so everyone could understand and apply the information.

"Are you saying we're all going to use the same list?" Becca asked.

David thought for a second and then answered, "I'm suggesting we should all want to use a similar list if in fact we all agree it is the standard we want to use in raising our kids into adulthood."

"That's great news," Becca replied with a gasp. "I was thinking each couple had to create our own list, and I was worried ours would be incomplete."

Hailey, who was sitting next to Becca, put her arm around her friend and said, "There is no doubt you and Scott could come up with an amazing list yourself, but that's what this group is for. Remember, Proverbs says, *As iron sharpens iron, so one person sharpens another.* That's what I love about you guys. You each make me better."

Becca, who appreciated the comments, gave Hailey a brief hug. In typical fashion Brian looked over to David and whispered, "We should hug more, buddy." David tried not to laugh, but he couldn't help it.

Jess, still in the moment of the parenting discussion, grabbed her Bible and flipped through it. "That reminds me of a verse," she said. "Where is it?" She finally stopped flipping. "Here it is. I love this verse." Then she read aloud Ecclesiastes 4:12. *Though one may be overpowered, two can defend themselves. A cord of three strands is not quickly broken.*

Everyone agreed that the verse was perfect for the group. "So with that perfect verse in mind, let's start," David said. "Once again, we are creating an agreed-upon list of qualities, traits, and characteristics we all want to eventually see instilled in our kids as they grow into adults—our parenting standard. Jess, do you mind writing these on the board?"

She jumped up. "Absolutely!" She walked over to the dry-erase board and wrote across the top in large bold letters, *We Want Our Kids to Become...*

David continued. "I don't exactly know how this is going to go, but here's what I had in mind. We will go around and share the lists we brought. Then we can ask questions, discuss each one, and maybe even explain why each is important. And then, only if we all agree, we put it on the board. Does that work for everyone?"

Everyone nodded, and Chris said, "No more delaying. Let's do this."

Hailey spoke up. "I will go first. I don't know if you would call this a trait or a quality, but it's one we have used with our boys for years. We tell them we want them to become godly young men. I guess we need to modify it to say 'men and women,' but we have been telling the boys this statement since they were old enough to talk."

"I was going to suggest the same thing, honey," David said to his wife. "She's right. We have said this to the boys forever. If you went downstairs right now and asked Noah what his parents' goal is for him, he would definitely say, 'To become a godly young man.'"

"Your kids are so young," Scott commented. "What's the point in saying this now? Do you think they will even remember as they get older?"

"Great question," David answered quickly as if he was expecting it. "Yes, I know they will remember it because we discuss it often. We want our kids to always know exactly what Hailey and I are trying to accomplish with them—our goal as parents as well as our expectations of them. We tell them this all the time."

"So you just say this randomly, or only at certain times?" Becca asked.

"Anytime and all the time," David answered. "Sometimes it's when they get punished, sometimes at night when we tuck them in bed, sometimes during a heart-to-heart talk, and sometimes completely random. The reason is we don't just want them to know *what* we want them to become, but we also want them to understand *why* we want this for them. We want them to know what we strive for as parents. Remember that quote I shared last week from Andy Andrews? Our desire is to ingrain in their minds that our purpose as parents is to prepare them for adulthood and not just to get through childhood. There's a huge difference."

Brian said, "I have been thinking about that quote all week. I'm embarrassed to admit it, but I have never thought about parenting like that before. I guess I am so focused on the kids' day-to-day lives that I haven't stopped to consider who they will be as adults...or at least who I hope they will be."

"My guess is most parents are the same," David replied. "They parent more for the moment than they do for the future. We used to be that way."

Hailey added, "By the way, we know the boys aren't going to be perfect. Our sincere prayer is that when Noah and Joseph are seventeen or eighteen years old, that people who see them will think, *Those are two godly young men.*"

"That's the kind of guy I want Caroline to marry one day," Jess agreed. She turned to the board and wrote, *#1—Godly young men and women.*

We Want Our Kids to Become...
#1—Godly young men and women

Everyone in the group, including David and Hailey, wrote the phrase down in their own notes. Even though they had just started, it felt like they had already made tremendous progress.

David said, "Does someone else want to share next? What is most important to you for your kids to become one day?"

Without hesitation and in unison, Chris, Brian, and Becca all said, "I'll share."

Brian said, "Ladies first," and the attention turned to Becca.

"Well, I think everyone agrees that we want our children to trust in Jesus," she said with confidence. "Nothing is more important to Scott and me than passing our Christian faith on to our kids. We talked about this more this week than all the other aspects. We greatly desire that the kids love Jesus and follow him wholeheartedly."

David partway raised his hand slightly and said, "I want to challenge one thing you said. While I couldn't agree with you more, unfortunately not all parents feel the same as we do. I'm referring to churchgoing parents."

"Who wouldn't want their kids to share their faith in Christ?" Becca asked, confused.

"If I really get going on this one, you want be able to shut me up," David joked, glancing over to Hailey. "Hailey will tell you—this is my hot button."

"Yeah, definitely don't get him started on this topic or we will be here all night," she jabbed at her husband.

David took a deep breath and calmly continued. "All I'll say is that I have met many parents in the church who don't think it's a priority to pass their faith on to their children. They are too concerned with being their kids' friend and then a parent. And many of them are too worried about forcing their kids to go to church or coming across as pushing their biblical faith on them, but they don't stop to consider the long-term and even eternal consequences of their kids not accepting their Christian faith." David stopped and then added, "Hailey and I completely agree with you, Becca. Nothing is as important to us as Noah and Joseph loving and living for Jesus."

"And also loving the Word of God," Scott said. "One main reason we homeschool the kids is because we couldn't afford to send them to a Christian school but wanted them to have a biblical foundation. So Becca chose to homeschool them so she could add Bible as a class subject, and she has done an incredible job teaching them. I'm so proud of her."

Scott looked at his wife, who was seated next to him, and grabbed her by the hand. For the first time in nearly two years, Scott showed a little emotion. His eyes turned pink and teared up. He put his head down for a moment, and then he lifted it back up and continued sharing. "We took a pretty big financial hit when she decided to stay home and teach. It was hard at first, but we figured it out. When I see how much those kids know about the Bible now and how much they enjoy learning the stories..." He got choked up again, so he stopped to gather himself. Then he simply said, "It's worth it."

Tears in her eyes, Jess turned back to the board and wrote, #2—*In love with Jesus and his Word.*

We Want Our Kids to Become...
#1—Godly young men and women
#2—In love with Jesus and his Word

Acting as facilitator, David asked, "Who else wants to share?"

Brian and Chris looked at each other. Chris gave Brian a nod, saying, "Go ahead."

Brian cocked his head back and talked with an over-the-top arrogant voice. "As a world-famous celebrity baseball coach and defending state champion..." He stopped, and everyone smiled as did he. He continued in a more serious tone. "I'm just kidding around. In all seriousness, as a baseball coach I realize I am known in the community for better or worse. Some people like me and some might not, but that's just part of being head coach of a successful program."

David asked, "By the way, when are we all getting free game tickets?" Brian laughed, but he didn't have a comeback. David said to his friend, "I'm just messing with you, buddy. Please, keep going."

"Ever since last Sunday, the same phrase has been bouncing around in my head," Brian told the group. *"A good name, a good name, a good name.* Really, I've been thinking about it all the time. You guys know I'm still fairly new to the Bible, so I went online and searched 'a good name.' The first result was the first verse of Proverbs twenty-two. Do you know that verse?" Brian looked at David.

David answered, *"A good name is more desirable than great riches; to be esteemed is better than silver or gold."*

"Exactly," Brian replied. "I memorized it, and when I think about the kind of men and women I want our kids to become one day, that's my answer. Wherever they live, I want them to have *a good name* in their community. And just like with a baseball coach, whether people like them or not, I want them to be respected by others."

"That's great," David said as the others also agreed. "I talk about this verse a lot with students, as well as what it means to have a good reputation. I try to keep it simple for them, so I always say that your reputation is what people think about when they think about you. So when people think about our children, whether it's teachers, coaches, or other students, something comes to their minds, right? I like the way you said it better, Brian." David looked around the room. "Are we all good with this one?"

Everyone unanimously agreed, so Jess walked back up to the board and wrote, *#3—Respected in their community.*

WE WANT OUR KIDS TO BECOME...
#1—Godly young men and women
#2—In love with Jesus and his Word
#3—Respected in their community

"While we are on the subject of respect, I want to dovetail off this one," Hailey shared. She looked down at the notes that she had prepared before the meeting. "I desperately want our boys to learn how to treat other people with respect. I love what you said, Brian, about having a good name worthy of respect in our community. But I also pray they will love and honor all other people regardless of who they are."

"Yeah, I agree. That's a good one," Brian said. "I can tell you from working in a high school that many teenagers don't treat other students with respect. Sometimes they can be downright mean and disgusting to anyone who doesn't look like them or run in their circles. It's sad actually."

"We experience that same dynamic at times in student ministry," Hailey added, "and that's with kids who actually come to church. I can't imagine how much worse it is at school. I'm sure David experiences it when he ministers on school campuses." She turned toward her husband. "I know you preach on it often."

"It's not only sad," David added, "but it's completely devastating. The amount of ridicule, teasing, and loneliness some students face at school breaks my heart. That's why we consider the school campus the largest mission field in America. I don't mean to get off subject here, but it's incredible the impact a Christian student can make on campus when making the conscious decision to truly love other students—simple stuff like sitting at lunch with a kid who always eats by himself, befriending someone who doesn't have many friends, or talking to kids who look different than those in their group." David looked at Hailey and laughed. "I'm sorry, honey. Here I go again, talking too much. You were sharing about our kids having respect for all others. Go ahead." Everyone else giggled, not to make fun of him but because David was known for going off on tangents. No one else minded, because he never interrupted others while they were talking. It was just that he usually had a lot to say—good wisdom and experiences to share. But it bothered him more than anyone else, because he didn't want to look like a talking head.

"No, you're fine," Hailey replied. "I was going to ask you to share about campus missionary stuff, so that's good. Anyway the words on my heart all week have been, 'respecting all people.' I pray we raise Noah and Joseph in such a way that when they are older they treat everyone with dignity and respect. We already teach this to the boys, but I hope it sticks."

"What are some things you have done to teaching the boys to have this quality?" Jess asked. By the tone of her voice, she wasn't just being conversational—she wanted guidance.

"We certainly haven't mastered this one yet," Hailey admitted, "but there are a few things we do often to instill this principle. David constantly reminds them that they aren't better than anyone else. What's that quote you use, David?"

He quickly answered. "You boys are no better than anyone else, and no one is better than you either. God makes us all special."

"I'm going to steal that quote and pretend I made it up," Brian said, writing it down.

Hailey shared a few more examples with Jess. "We try to teach by using real-life scenarios. One time we were at a restaurant, and the people next to us were being very rude to their young waitress. When the manager came over to see them, they spoke to him with kindness. I took that opportunity to ask the boys what they noticed about the situation. I was able to talk about how Christians should respect everyone, no matter people's age or how much money they make."

Another memory popped into Hailey's head. "Oh, and another time we were at Noah's baseball game, and a parent yelled at the umpire. They had to stop the game, and the umpire threw this mom out. I didn't even know fans could get thrown out. Then the two head coaches yelled at each other from across the field. It was crazy. The kids were only eight years old, and the adults were acting like it was the World Series."

"Amen to that sister," Brian shouted.

Hailey laughed and said, "Immediately after the game when we were in the car, David had a long conversation with Noah about what happened. He talked about how wrong it was for that mother to disrespect the umpire, even though he did make a bad call. He explained that it was even worse for the two coaches to disrespect each other and set a bad example in front of the kids. To our surprise, Noah completely got it."

Hailey looked up at Jess, who was still standing next to the dry-erase board, and concluded, "We just look for teachable moments. I think the most important way for us all to imprint this quality into our kids, though, is to live it out ourselves. We must first treat all people with dignity and respect, whether we feel that they deserve it or not. Especially if we want to reach people who are not like us and win them to Jesus."

Jess stood for a moment in deep thought as she listened to Hailey. She didn't say it, but she knew she had some work to do with parenting her own daughter. At the same time, she was thankful she still had a few more years with her fifteen-year-old. It wasn't too late. Jess managed a quick smile and then said, "That's a good one, Hailey. I needed that." Then Jess wrote down, *#4—Respectful to all people.*

We Want Our Kids to Become…
#1—Godly young men and women
#2—In love with Jesus and his Word
#3—Respected in their community
#4—Respectful to all people

It was getting late, so the group decided to call it a night. Everyone was excited about how much they had accomplished together in an hour. It was the closest they had ever been together. This group of four couples was starting to act like one. It was beautiful. It was the church. On the drive home, David thought about what the first-century church must have been like. He couldn't recall the exact verse. After he and Hailey got home, he went into his office and opened his Bible to Acts 2:44:

All the believers were together and had everything in common.

CHAPTER TEN

"Hey, sweetheart, can I come in?" Chris stood at his stepdaughter's open bedroom door.

"Sure, Dad, what's up?" Caroline answered, although she never looked up. She was on her bed, doing homework and listening to music.

"Can you please turn the music down for a minute?" he asked. "I want to talk to you."

Sensing his serious tone, Caroline turned the music off, closed her books, and sat up straight. "Is everything OK, Dad?"

"Oh, yeah, baby girl, everything is fine." Chris sat down on the edge of Caroline's bed. "You have just been on my mind a lot lately. I've been thinking about some things and, well, I guess actually I'm changing the way I think about those things—you know, trying to take certain things more seriously." Chris stopped talking, because he realized his words were not coming out right. He was stuttering and unsure of himself.

He and Caroline had always had a pretty good relationship, since he and Jess got married. He loved her just like she were his own, and she treated him as if he were her real father. But for some reason, they weren't as close as Chris wanted them to be, especially in the last couple of years since she became a teenager. She had become more distant and private, and so Chris, not knowing how to respond, gave her too much space and separation. She was a good girl, very committed to church and her relationship with Jesus. But recently she became more rebellious, and her attitude was horrible, especially with her mother. She and Jess were so much alike that they argued way too often. Chris always felt insecure with his roles and responsibility as a stepfather and husband. He didn't want to choose sides, so he did something much worse—he mentally and emotionally retreated from them both. Jess needed him to be a supportive husband, and Caroline needed an understanding father, but he knew he had been neither. However, since they had ventured into this parenting topic in small group, Chris was now ready to become the man of the house he knew God wanted him to be.

Caroline looked confused as Chris struggled for the right words. He prayed before he walked into her room, asking God to give him wisdom in speaking with her, but he felt lost and blank. Chris took a deep breath, prayed a quick prayer in his head, grabbed Caroline by the hand, and started over. "What I'm trying to say, Caroline, is that I love you," he began.

"I love you too, Daddy," his stepdaughter said with a smile.

"I have been convicted recently that I have not been a great father to you, or at least not the father God wants me to be. I know you need me more now than ever before, but I have neglected you in so many ways. Not on purpose," he assured her, squeezing her hand tighter, "but I am concerned that my failure as a father is showing itself in the way you behave lately in your attitude toward your mother."

"But, Dad, she—"

Chris cut her off. "Honey, I am not here to reprimand you. You are not in trouble. I just want to tell you I am sorry. From now on I will be a more involved and committed father for you. You deserve that."

Caroline stared, speechless, at her stepfather. She didn't know exactly how to respond. She was used to being accused of something and then defending herself. She had become quite talented at arguing and proving her point, but she didn't know how to reply to her father's confession.

"I also want to tell you something you might not know about your mom. Did you know your mother used to be considered one of the most beautiful women in town?" Chris smiled, and so did Caroline. "It's true. When I first met her, you were very young. I was intimidated because she was so gorgeous. And you know what?"

"What?" Caroline answered.

"You look just like her." Caroline smiled even bigger and then looked down bashfully.

"Here's the truth, baby," Chris said, wrapping his arm around her. "You know what attracted me to her even more than looks?" Caroline didn't answer but looked up into his eyes. "I was attracted to who she was. I was attracted to her reputation and her good name. You see, darling, looks can come and go, but your mother had a reputation as being one of the best girls around. She loved the Lord, she dressed modestly, and she behaved honorably. God completely changed her life when she got saved. The reputation she had in high school fell away. Now she was known as a hot girl on fire for Jesus!" Caroline laughed, and Chris joined in.

After a few seconds, Chris said, "Caroline, you are even more beautiful than she was. I know you love the Lord with all your heart, so here is the decision you face. Which reputation do you want for yourself? Do you want to be known as your mother was in high school? Or do you want to be known in this community for having the reputation your mother did when I met her? Your name is important, sweetheart. Your name is important to God, and it's important to me. I hope it's important to you as well."

Tears flowed down Caroline's cheeks. She stared deep into her father's eyes, as if he had just given her new life. With his arm still around his little girl, Chris asked, "Do you understand what I'm saying?"

"Yes, Daddy," she answered, crying harder. "I understand." Caroline put her head in her stepfather's chest and wept. Chris held her, rocking back and forth. In his mind, he said over and over again, *Thank you, Jesus. Thank you, Jesus. Thank you, Jesus.*

"Can you guys believe that?" Chris asked after sharing his story with the small group the following week. "It was one of the most special moments of my life. The best part is that ever since that conversation, Caroline is like a new girl. She comes out of her room and hangs out with us, and her attitude toward Jess is so much better. It's a breakthrough, David, and we have been thanking God all week."

There wasn't a dry eye in the room. Everyone responded by sharing feelings and congratulating Chris and Jess on their massive steps forward with their daughter.

"I was so convicted and yet, at the same time, motivated after our small group last week. This is good stuff." Chris swept the tears from his cheeks and gained composure.

David regained everyone's attention. "Thanks, Chris, for sharing that story. We pray that more events like that occur in all our families as we implement these parenting strategies. Like we've said before, the goal is to raise godly young men and women. In order to do that, we must first know whom exactly we are trying to raise. Then we should be intentional and purposeful in how to raise that type of young man or woman."

Everyone agreed. By now, the entire group of eight individuals was not only one the same page, but they were in sync. They were totally bought in to the idea of what David was teaching, and in fact, they were all acting as teachers to one another.

David continued. "So far we have identified four qualities and traits we all want to see lived out in our children as they grow into adults. We have all been thinking and praying about what to add to this list, so who wants to share now?"

"I can share mine real quick, if no one minds." It was Leslie. "I actually only have one quality on my list, so this won't take long. I think the most important trait for me to see in our family is humility."

"Exactly," Brian blurted out. "I think everyone should be as humble as I am." After a quick laugh, he turned to his wife. "I'm just kidding, honey. Go ahead. I'm sorry." Leslie was so used to Brian's sarcasm and goofiness that she didn't even skip a beat as she continued to share. "I think one of the most attractive qualities of any person is humility. Actually, I can't think of a more disgusting characteristic than that of an arrogant, egotistical person."

"I completely agree," Hailey replied. "I have humility on my list as well."

"So do I. That's a great one, Leslie," David affirmed.

"Brian and I talk about it a lot with our kids," Leslie continued. "Believe it or not, Brian is actually a really humble guy." She lightly slapped her husband in the back of the head. "He plays around a lot, but he is very humble."

Brian smiled at the compliment.

"If I may brag on him for a second," Leslie said, "with all of his success as a baseball coach, he never takes himself too seriously. That's one thing I love most about him. We talk about it at home because, as you guys know, both our kids are pretty good athletes. They are head and shoulders above everyone else on their baseball and swim teams. Sometimes they tend to become a bit cocky since all the other kids always tell them how great they are."

"They were certainly born with God-given gifts," David agreed.

"Thank you, and we know that," Leslie replied, "but it's very important for us to teach them to remain humble, even if they are good. Some of their competitive teammates just think they are God's gift to the world. It drives us crazy.

What's even worse than their arrogance is their parents. They genuinely think their kids hung the moon." Brian interrupted. "Yeah, the more we are around certain kids and parents, the more we come to realize how negative a trait egotism is and how positive humility is."

The dry-erase board already had four qualities written down, but Jess walked over and added the fifth: *Humble at all times.*

We Want Our Kids to Become...
#1—Godly young men and women
#2—In love with Jesus and his Word
#3—Respected in their community
#4—Respectful to all people
#5—Humble at all times

"I have another good one to share," David said. "I realize this is gender-specific, but let me explain why it should be included in our parenting standard."

"Our first controversy," Brian laughed. "I have a feeling this will be fun."

"It's not controversial, man." David smiled and shook his head at his friend. "It just needs to be clarified. But here it is first, and then we can discuss it. Hailey and I teach our boys to treat women with honor."

At the exact same time, Becca, Leslie, and Jess smiled and nodded in support.

David continued. "I realize we have two boys and that some of you have girls. I am also fully aware that our goal is to create an agreed-upon list of qualities and traits we can all use in raising our children into adulthood. At first glance it might seem like this would only apply to raising boys. But Hailey and I strongly agree that both boys and girls, and ultimately men and women, should understand what it means to treat women with honor. In the case of your daughters, they need to know what it looks like to be treated with honor by a man. Young ladies should always expect to be treated with honor and respect. Does that make sense?"

"Absolutely, buddy," Chris said. "It's just as important that Caroline understands how a man should treat her as it is that Noah and Joseph should learn how to treat a lady."

"Exactly right!" said Hailey. "Does everyone agree that chivalry is almost dead in America?"

"Amen, sister! Brian, write that down." Leslie slapped her husband's leg.

"As you all know, gender is a hot topic in recent years." David paused as if trying to decide how to proceed. "While our culture has decided gender means absolutely nothing anymore, we all know Scripture says otherwise. God made us in his image, but he also made us uniquely." David pointed at himself and Hailey. "Hailey and I made the decision long ago that our job isn't to raise our kids based on culture or popular opinion. Rather, our job as Christian parents is to raise our children according to God's holy Word and the eternal truths of Scripture."

David looked back and forth at Scott, Brian, and Chris. "It is imperative, guys, that we teach our boys what it means to be men. It is equally imperative that we teach them to honor women. We need to bring chivalry back, and it starts with how we treat our wives. This lesson of honoring women will be better caught than taught."

None of the wives dared say a word, as this was no time for a joke or funny comment. Likewise, none of the men responded with words. Instead they all looked to David in silence, like athletes who had just received a play call from their coach. After several quiet seconds, David broke the ice. "I failed at this miserably during our first few years of marriage," he admitted. "I'm thankful my kids weren't around yet to witness it. I used to act disrespectfully toward Hailey, even putting her down in public. I was driving a wedge in my own marriage, without even realizing it. God convicted me of my spiritual immaturity. Over the last several years, he has been teaching me what it means to be a man and how I should treat my wife, how I should honor her. And now he is showing me the importance of teaching my boys to honor their future wives."

"When David teaches teenagers, he says one phrase over and over," Hailey added. "'Never settle for less than God's best for your life,' he tells them. I've heard him say this line a thousand times over the years. One problem we see with teenagers and college students is that many are never taught how to properly treat a member of the opposite sex. Nor have they been shown what it looks like to be treated respectfully by a man or woman. Many of them settle for far less than God's desired best for their lives."

Jess stood and headed for the board. She looked over toward David and Hailey and said, "I just love you guys. I'm so glad we are in this group together." Then she wrote down, *#6—Honoring toward women.*

We Want Our Kids to Become...
#1—Godly young men and women
#2—In love with Jesus and his Word
#3—Respected in their community
#4—Respectful to all people
#5—Humble at all times
#6—Honoring toward women

Still writing on the board with her back to the group, Jess said, "I would like to share a quality that is at the top of my list." She turned around to see if anyone objected. When she realized she had the floor, she said, "Character and integrity." She hurried back to her seat and grabbed her notebook. "I wrote a few things down," she said joyfully.

As Jess was glancing through her notes, everyone else in the group wrote on their papers, *Character and integrity.*

"OK, here it is," Jess said. She picked up her Bible. "I want to read a passage from Daniel, chapter six. I was reading this a couple weeks ago, when I was creating my list for this discussion. Daniel might be the perfect example of what it looks like for a Christian to live each day with integrity, whether life is easy or difficult."

"Which chapter and verse?" Scott asked.

"Daniel, chapter six, and I'm going to read verses three through five," Jess answered. After waiting for everyone to find the passage, she read.

Now Daniel so distinguished himself among the administrators and the satraps by his exceptional qualities that the king planned to set him over the whole kingdom. At this, the administrators and the satraps tried to find grounds for charges against Daniel in his conduct of government affairs, but they were unable to do so. They could find no corruption in him, because he was trustworthy and neither corrupt nor negligent. Finally these men said, "We will never find any basis for charges against this man Daniel unless it has something to do with the law of his God."

"Wow, I love that," Brian remarked. "I have never read that passage before. I have heard of Daniel and the lion's den, but that's really all I remember about Daniel."

David smiled at the young believer, "Yeah, Daniel was the man—probably the best example of integrity in the entire Bible, other than Jesus of course. That's a great passage, Jess."

"I know, right?" she said with excitement. "I couldn't wait to share it with everyone because I think it perfectly illustrates everything we are trying to accomplish with our kids. Think about it: to be able to raise young adult children similar to Daniel. That would just be..." She couldn't think of the right word.

"The goal." David finished her sentence.

"Yes, the goal," Jess agreed.

"Again, that is exactly the point of what we are doing here," David elaborated. "As Christian parents, we need to have a goal for who our children will become as adults. We don't just hope they will one day have integrity and character. We must purposefully and intentionally teach and model integrity to them. We must choose to live our own lives with integrity. The words 'character' and 'integrity' should be ever-present in our language, lessons, and teaching."

Jess hopped back over to the board. "Everyone agrees to add it to the list?"

"Absolutely," Becca agreed.

"Yeah, that one is so important," Hailey added. "Thank you, Jess."

Jess grabbed her dry-erase marker and wrote, #7—*Full of character and integrity.*

We Want Our Kids to Become…
#1—Godly young men and women
#2—In love with Jesus and his Word
#3—Respected in their community
#4—Respectful to all people
#5—Humble at all times
#6—Honoring toward women
#7—Full of character and integrity

"OK, we probably have time for one more," David said.

Becca leaned over to toward her husband and pointed at her watch. Scott knew exactly what that meant. "I'm sorry, but we have to leave a few minutes early tonight," he said bashfully. "We procrastinated over the weekend, so we didn't finish our homework."

Ever quick on his toes, Brian asked, "You still have to do homework, Scott?"

Scott laughed, realizing how silly that sounded. "No, actually I don't have homework. A couple of our kids do."

Becca placed her hand lovingly on her husband's leg. "Let's just say *someone* was in charge of helping the kids with their homework on Friday, and *someone* didn't make them finish it, so *someone* has to go home and help them get it done."

Everyone laughed, not because it was that funny, but because they had all been there before and could relate. "Sounds to me like *someone* is in trouble," Brian said, looking at Scott and smiling.

"Yeah, yeah, I know." Scott grinned. "Before we go, I would like to quickly share one of the most important qualities on my list for our kids. If we need to wait until next week to decide if we want to add it to our standard or not, that's perfectly fine."

"Sure, buddy, go for it," David replied.

"I will be brief and to the point," Scott said. "Maybe because it's how I was raised, but a hard-work ethic is at the top of my list. If there is anything I want our kids to have, it's the ability to work hard."

"Hear, hear!" Chris exclaimed.

Scott appreciated the support. "I was raised to believe a person can get anywhere in life if he or she is willing to work hard enough for it. As a young child, I was required to do chores and work around the house. We didn't get an allowance, of course. My dad used to say, 'You are allowed to live here for free; that's your allowance.' I got my first summer job when I was thirteen, and I worked part time all the way through high school. I put myself through college by working nights and weekends while my friends partied. Even though we have been very blessed in our insurance agency, my partner and I worked our tails off to make it. I have never stopped working hard for my clients and for my family."

Scott suddenly realized he had been talking for several minutes. Everyone was listening intently. It was by far the longest Scott had ever talked in two years of coming to this group. David was completely focused on everything Scott said, but at the same time, he couldn't help reflecting on how dramatically Scott had changed. Scott used to be quiet, closed off, and skeptical. Now he was open, engaging, and relational. It was a beautiful transformation. *This is what small group is all about*, David thought.

"I don't mean to talk too much," Scott said apologetically.

"No, no, please go on." David looked at Scott and smiled. "Scott, I love what you said. I have work ethic on my list as well. I think it's so important parents do a better job of instilling a hard-work ethic in their kids. I see the wrong side of it sometimes in student ministry. So many teenagers in our church feel entitled to everything. They have no idea what real work is, but they expect their parents to just give them whatever they want. Unfortunately, many parents comply to their demands."

"It drives me crazy," Scott admitted. "I don't know how you are around it so often without saying anything."

David answered, "I have learned there is only so much I can do. I can teach what the Bible says, I can give advice or counsel when parents ask me, and I can teach my own children. But honestly, that's about it. If I tried to pry in people's personal lives, I wouldn't last very long at this church. They would get rid of me quickly." David laughed.

"Yeah, I guess that makes sense," Scott replied.

"That's actually why I love what we are trying to accomplish and why what we are doing is so important." David leaned up on the edge of his seat. "Do you realize how rare you are, or how rare it is to do this?" David slowly looked around the room. "Very few people take the time to do what we are seeking to do. Very few learn how to think differently about parenting. It's not just about making it through life and hoping our 'good' kids turn out well. It's about being intentional and parenting on purpose."

David turned to Chris and asked, "Chris, what are your thoughts on this? You are very successful in your career, and you work as hard as anyone I know."

Without hesitation, Chris answered, "Well, I would like to add one thought. In addition to instilling work ethic, it's also important to teach kids what it means to be an entrepreneur. Instead of just studying in school to get a job one day, they can learn to create opportunities. Yes, I admit I am somewhat of a workaholic, but I attribute our success more to my entrepreneurial spirit than anything else. So it's working hard, working smart, and at the same time, learning to spot opportunities. That's my two cents."

"Well said," Scott replied. He looked over at Becca, who was giving him *the look*. "OK, we really need to go now. I know that look." Becca smiled, and they both stood to leave.

Jess quickly ran over to the board. "OK, OK, just one second," she said. "Let me write this down first before you go. I'm too obsessive-compulsive to leave the board blank until next Sunday." She wrote, *#8—Hardworking and entrepreneurial.*

We Want Our Kids to Become...
#1—Godly young men and women
#2—In love with Jesus and his Word
#3—Respected in their community
#4—Respectful to all people
#5—Humble at all times
#6—Honoring toward women
#7—Full of character and integrity
#8—Hardworking and entrepreneurial

CHAPTER ELEVEN

It was Thursday at 2:45 p.m. when Hailey pulled into the school parking lot. She was about to begin her daily thirty-minute routine of waiting in a long car line to pick up the boys from school. She loved picking them up and talking about their days, but she dreaded the long wait in line every day. She usually used this as an opportunity to return phone calls, check her e-mail, or kill time on Facebook. Just as she was about to pick up her phone, it rang. It was Becca. "Hey girl," Hailey said.

"Hello, Hailey. How are you?" Becca asked.

"I'm blessed and doing just fine. How are you today? What's going on?"

"Oh, we are doing wonderful as well," Becca said. "We just finished our schoolwork, and now the kids are outside playing."

"I still don't know how you homeschool four children every day. You are amazing! I would go crazy." Hailey laughed, as did Becca.

Becca asked, "Am I catching you at a bad time? I just have a quick question."

"No, this is perfect timing," Hailey replied. "I just got in line to pick up the boys, so I have thirty minutes free."

"OK, good," Becca said. "Scott and I have been talking this week about last Sunday night. We really enjoy this parenting discussion. We have both already learned so much. I want to ask you about your kids. David talked last week about teaching your boys how to treat women with honor. Scott and I feel we have not done a great job with that so far, but we want to make it a priority. Will you share a few specific things you and David do with Noah and Joseph to drive that lesson home?"

"Absolutely, I would love to share a few ideas with you," Hailey responded with excitement. "First I want to say that there is nothing special about what we have done with our boys. There are many things we need to do better. But if there is one thing we do well, it's just staying consistent."

"Girl, you don't have to be humble or modest," Becca interrupted. "I know you guys aren't perfect, but you and David are incredible parents. Your boys are two of the best kids I've ever been around, so you are doing something right. I would like to teach our kids to honor and respect women, so anything you can share with me would be great— just a few specific things you guys do."

"You are too kind," Hailey humbly countered. "Hmm, let me think." Hailey paused, trying to think of what would be helpful. "Oh, I just thought of something. It's small, but I think it's what you are asking."

Becca said, "I'm all ears. I just need a few examples."

"I'll tell you a quick story, which I think you will appreciate." Hailey began, "Last Friday night the four of us went out to dinner. After parking the car, David walked around and opened my door for me. He didn't say a word, but the boys always notice. As we walked, he held my hand the whole way. When we got to the entrance of the restaurant, Noah held the door open for us all. When the waitress took us to our seats, Noah attempted to help me to my chair. He couldn't actually push the chair with me sitting in it, but he tried. Maybe I just need to lose a few pounds." They both laughed. Hailey continued, "When we ordered our food, they let me go first of course, but that's normal. Finally, during the meal, I had to get up and go to the bathroom. When I got back to the table, David and both boys stood up until I sat down. David had to remind Joseph, but he is getting better."

"Wow!" Becca whispered, half to herself and half to Hailey.

"Please don't think too highly of us," Hailey quickly added. "The boys don't always do that well, including David. We have to remind the kids often to do these things. My point in sharing that story is that we try our best to consistently teach and model what it means for them to honor women. They don't always get it right, but it's always on the forefront of our minds and it comes up often in our conversations. The boys learn by first watching how David treats me but also by our intentional effort to teach and explain chivalry and honor." Hailey waited on a response, but she heard nothing on the other end. "Becca, are you still there?"

"Oh, yes, sorry," she answered. "I was just writing down what you said."

"Please don't get me wrong, girl. They don't always do those things," Hailey said. "They did really well that night, but we usually have to remind them often. Our goal is to instill these things in them now, so they become second nature by the time they are teenagers and beyond."

"That's wonderful. I love that story," Becca replied. "Thanks for your time."

"Girl, anytime," Hailey said. "Oh, and here is the best part of that story. Apparently a senior adult couple in the restaurant saw how the boys treated me, so they anonymously picked up our check and bought our dinner. The waitress wouldn't tell us who it was. All she told us was that an elderly couple appreciated how respectful our boys were."

"That is so special. Scott will love that story," Becca said.

"You know David loved it. Anything to save a dollar!" They both laughed before hanging up.

When Sunday night arrived, all four couples gathered once again in the living room at the Clines' home. For the third week in a row, the ladies didn't congregate in the kitchen to talk about life for twenty minutes, nor did the guys even mention sports or politics. Everyone was on time and went straight to their seats, ready to start. They only had about ninety minutes together each week, so they wanted to make each second count. Even Brian, who normally had a random funny story to share, sat with his Bible, notebook, and pen in hand.

David looked at Brian and said, "Hey, buddy, would you be willing to open us up with a quick prayer?" David knew

Brian had never prayed out loud since joining the group. He was putting him on the spot, but he felt like it was time. Brian was caught off guard. David quietly nodded at him as if to say, "You can do it."

Brian hesitated for a second, but then replied, "Sure." He bowed his head and prayed, "Dear Lord, I love you so much. Thank you for loving me and forgiving my many sins. Lord, we all want to become better parents. Would you please teach us how? And thank you for this group of friends. I don't know where I would be right now if not for them. Amen."

"Amen. Thank you, Brian. That was perfect," David affirmed.

Jess jumped up and said, "Oops, I forgot to set it out." She ran out of the room and quickly returned with the dry-erase board. "There," she said. "Now we can begin."

David started the discussion. "I don't know how many we will end up with at the end, but we currently have identified eight qualities and characteristics we want to see lived out in our adult children. I still have a couple to share, and I know several of you do as well. If it's all right, I will go first." Everyone grabbed his or her notes. "Anyone who knows me knows how important this one is to me, but one quality I would like to add to the list is manners. This is definitely a soapbox moment for me, so I will try to contain myself," David said with a sneaky grin.

"Good luck with that, honey," Hailey said with a smile. "Someone start the timer."

"Ha-ha," he replied to his wife. "I can just feel the love tonight."

"I'm just playing," Hailey teased. "We all know how important good manners are to you."

"It is important to me," David said. He sat up on the edge of his seat. "I'm preaching to the choir here, but let me say one simple truth about good manners."

"Say all you want," Chris said.

"The importance of great manners is not what many people think," David continued. "Many parents think it's all about creating these polite little children they can show off to their friends. As if saying 'please' and 'thank you' makes someone a good kid. It doesn't. Some of the most polite teenagers I've ever had turned out to be the most manipulative. But this is what is important to me as a father. This is the real truth about good manners."

The group could see in his eyes that he was about to say something important. It was more than a look of passion and excitement; it was truth and wisdom. "People with good manners aren't necessarily better people," David explained, "but they definitely have a greater advantage over those who don't. That's the truth, and that's what I teach my kids. It's not that I just want them to be sweet and nice; I want them to maintain an advantage in every area of their lives. I guarantee you that well-mannered people are more respected than those who are not. With more respect comes greater advantage."

David looked around to see if he had lost everyone with his passion. No one was looking at him, including Hailey. They were all looking down, writing as fast as they could. Realizing he wasn't annoying the group, he continued. "Our job as parents is to instill good manners into our children at their very core. We shouldn't simply give them a few words to repeat. We need to help them understand that it's about who they are becoming and why it's important. Good manners can give them an advantage in every area of life. If they use good manners with their schoolteachers, they will be more likely to receive extra help when needed. If they use good manners with police offers, they will be more likely to receive grace in a time of trouble. Brian, when you have players who not only work hard but also respect you by using good manners, are you not more likely to give them extra attention and focus?"

"Absolutely," he agreed. "I would bend over backward to help a player like that. In fact, I have two brothers on my team who I stay with after practice and help them with technique. They are two of the most polite and respectful boys I've ever coached. I guess I never thought about how much I appreciate that about them."

"Exactly," David responded. "Those boys have an advantage, not because of their talent but because of their manners and attitude. And what about future job interviews and relationships with employers? Think of the advantage our kids will have in career situations when they are polite, respectful, and well mannered. Chris, you hire tons of people. If you have two equal resumes, are you not more likely to hire the man or woman who wows you with respect and good manners?"

"One hundred percent of the time," Chris agreed.

"Don't get me started on dating." David laughed out loud. "I want my boys to end up with the two best wives on the planet. That won't happen by good looks alone." He gestured to himself as if he to indicate how handsome he was.

Everyone laughed, and David sat back in his chair. He had made his point and didn't want to ramble on too much. Brian poked at his friend. "Why don't you tell us how you really feel?"

"All joking aside, I have never thought about manners from the perspective of an advantage," Scott said. "We teach our children manners, but to be honest, it's probably more about making us look good than the advantages it can add to their lives. That's a completely new perspective."

"Yes, it is," David said.

"Great stuff, buddy," Chris added.

"That makes complete sense to me." Jess stood. "I don't think we need further discussion." She walked over to the board and wrote, *#9—Well-mannered.*

We Want Our Kids to Become...
#1—Godly young men and women
#2—In love with Jesus and his Word
#3—Respected in their community
#4—Respectful to all people
#5—Humble at all times
#6—Honoring toward women
#7—Full of character and integrity
#8—Hardworking and entrepreneurial
#9—Well-mannered

David said, "Who would like to suggest our next trait for the master list?"

"I only have one more on my list," Brian said. "I don't know if you guys will agree with this one. I know that you will think it's important, but whether or not we all want to add it to the final list is up to you. I'm good either way."

"What is it?" Hailey asked.

"Submissive to authority," he answered, "or submission to authorities—however you say it."

"Yeah, that's a great one," Hailey replied. David nodded in support as he wrote it in his notes.

"I think I know what you mean, but can you elaborate on why you think it's so important?" Becca asked.

"Sure," Brian replied. "I don't mean to sound like an old man, but it seems these younger generations have so little respect for authority. I've seen it worsen, just in the last fifteen years I have been teaching and coaching. You know, David—you work with teenagers. Most don't have that healthy fear of adults we did growing up. Actually, *reverence* might be the better word."

"Yes, I know exactly what you mean," David agreed. "A fifteen-year-old girl in my student ministry is the worst I've ever seen. Her name is Caroline." David smiled as Chris and Jess laughed.

"I'm not trying to sound negative toward teenagers. I love teaching and coaching," Brian continued. "But the more I see and hear at school and on the ball field, the more convicted I am to make sure my two kids turn out better. I don't mean that they are better people." Brian paused and tried to explain himself. "I just want my kids to be reverent and respectful to the authorities in their lives."

"Good point, buddy. The Bible has much to say about this subject," David said.

"Yeah, that's what I'm learning," Brian replied. He looked around at everyone and said, "I'm not as good at explaining things, but along the same lines as David was saying about manners giving kids an advantage in life, I also think teenagers and young adults who are respectful to authority stand out in our world. It's just so uncommon to see anymore."

Everyone unanimously agreed. "Brian, you're right," Hailey said. "It is uncommon to see kids, teenagers, and college-age students who are submissive to the authorities in their lives. We see it all the time when some students disrespect their parents even in public. I could tell you stories of times when students have mouthed off to David or blatantly disobeyed his rules. It's unbelievable."

"My father always said, 'It all comes back to parenting.' Every year I get older, the more I realize how right he was," David expressed. "I agree, Brian, that this one should go on our list. You are also right that people who respect their authorities stand out in a positive way. I tell my boys they will always have authorities in their lives—always. Whether it's their parents, teachers, coaches, pastors, bosses, or police officers. No matter how old they are or how successful they become, they will always be under someone's authority."

"Most important," Hailey added, "is that we teach our kids to be submissive to their greatest authority, their heavenly Father."

"Oh, that's good. I like that. I need to write that down," Jess exclaimed. "Are we good on this one?" Everyone gave it the go-ahead, so Jess went back to the board and wrote, *#10—Submissive to authority.*

We Want Our Kids to Become…
#1—Godly young men and women
#2—In love with Jesus and his Word
#3—Respected in their community
#4—Respectful to all people
#5—Humble at all times
#6—Honoring toward women
#7—Full of character and integrity
#8—Hardworking and entrepreneurial
#9—Well-mannered
#10—Submissive to authority

Chris looked at his watch. It was 7:08 p.m. "Do I have time to share one that is important to me?" he asked.

"We're at your house, buddy. We are all going to stay until you kick us out," Brian shot back.

"Great, I'll make this quick," Chris said. "Maybe it's the financial planner in me, but I think we need to add *wisdom with money* to our parenting standard. When I look at our list so far on the board, these qualities and traits are all so crucial. We all agree that many things in life are more important than money. However, when I consider the practicality of it, what is more valuable to a young adult than knowing how to handle money? Or what could be more devastating to the life of a young adult than *not* knowing how to properly manage finances?"

"Now you're speaking my language," David said, sitting up straight in his chair. "I can't wait to hear what you have to say."

"Me, too," Brian said. "I want some money." Everyone laughed at Brian's witty humor.

Chris indulged Brian's comment. "I don't want to talk about making money but about being good stewards of the money and resources God entrusts to us. I could bore you guys with all kinds of stats about how most families struggle financially. If you have ever listened to Dave Ramsey's radio show or attended one of his events, you know what I'm talking about. The sad truth is that a very small percentage of people manage their finances wisely. And wouldn't that logically mean that they probably aren't teaching their kids wise money lessons either?"

Dave said, "Whenever I reach at church about biblical stewardship or what the Bible says about money, most students look at me like I'm speaking a foreign language. All they know is making money and spending money...and if you don't have enough money, then just borrow more."

"Indeed," Chris agreed.

"Indeed!" Brian said with an exaggerated voice. "I haven't heard that word in a long time."

Chris shook his head. "I don't know what we are going to do with you, Brian." Chris changed back to a more serious tone and continued. "I am not talking about teaching our children to become savvy investors or build wealth. When I talk to clients or read statistics, it is obvious to me that most families never teach their kids how to handle money. So when their kids become adults, they naturally make unwise decisions. They spend more than they make, go into debt, don't save, and rarely give. I want more for my daughter than this sad reality, don't you guys?"

Every person nodded, but no one spoke up. A few seconds of awkward silence ensued. Having taught financial stewardship classes at church, David had experienced this before. Money was always a sore subject to discuss. No one wanted to admit it when they didn't have a clue as to what to do with their money, nor did anyone want to acknowledge when they were struggling financially. Instead of breaking the tension in the room, David chose to stay quiet and see what would happen.

Finally, Becca spoke up. "Chris, this all sounds great. I definitely agree with you that it's beneficial to teach our four children about money. I certainly want them to be better off one day than we are." She looked over at Scott to make sure she wasn't going too far in sharing their private financial affairs. He didn't seem to mind, so she continued. "What do we do when we don't know how to teach them about finances?"

Chris was not only an astute investor, but he was also a gifted financial counselor. He was more than prepared for Becca's question. "Becca, the real answer to that question would take quite some time to explain. Now is probably not the right time for that. However, it really doesn't take that much time and effort to learn a few things. Again, all I'm suggesting is that we teach our children to be wise with money—not savvy investors or Wall Street gurus. You can read a couple of good books or attend a seminar or class and be way ahead of the game in a matter of weeks. But more important, you will be prepared to pass on your newfound knowledge to your children so they are better prepared to enter into adulthood."

"What books do you recommend?" Scott asked.

"To start, anything by Dave Ramsey is great," Chris answered. "*The Total Money Makeover* and *Smart Money Smart Kids* are both very beneficial to helping any family with personal finances and teaching kids about money."

"I read both books, and they are great," David said. "Our church is hosting a Financial Peace University class in the spring. Those are really good too."

"Yeah, we have talked about doing that class before but just never committed," Becca admitted.

"When we finish up this parenting topic, maybe it would be a good idea to do a money thing next," David said. "Chris, you wouldn't mind leading that, would you?"

"That would be great," he responded.

David looked at his watch. They were now well beyond the ninety minutes. "It's getting late, so let's wrap this up," he said. "Jess, will you please write that one on the board?"

She walked over to the board and began to write, but then she stopped. "How do I word that one?" she asked.

Everyone looked at David for the answer, but he looked at Chris. "Wise stewards with money," Chris suggested.

With no objections, Jess wrote on the board, *#11—Wise stewards with money.*

We Want Our Kids to Become...
#1—Godly young men and women
#2—In love with Jesus and his Word
#3—Respected in their community
#4—Respectful to all people
#5—Humble at all times
#6—Honoring toward women
#7—Full of character and integrity
#8—Hardworking and entrepreneurial
#9—Well-mannered
#10—Submissive to authority
#11—Wise stewards with money

Before everyone got up to leave, David asked, "Does anyone have more on your personal list that we haven't yet covered?"

Jess and Hailey both raised their hands. "I do too," David said. "I guess we will go one more week with this discussion. I love you guys. Have a blessed week."

CHAPTER TWELVE

It was Sunday morning, and church had just dismissed. David, Hailey, Noah, and Joseph walked to their car to go home. Suddenly they heard a loud voice. David turned to see Brian waving his arms and lightly jogging toward them. He said, "Hey, buddy, I was trying to catch you before you took off."

"Are you breathing that hard from that little jog?" David joked.

"I know, right?" Brian laughed. "That's pathetic." Brian made small talk with Hailey and the boys, who then got in the car to wait on the men to talk.

"What's up, man?" David asked.

"This will only take a second," he said. "I have been thinking a lot about what Chris said last Sunday at group. Actually, Leslie and I have discussed it on three different occasions. We both feel convicted that we have not done an adequate job so far of teaching our kids about money. We are blessed with good incomes and manage our finances pretty well."

"Good incomes!" David said. "That's because you married a pharmacist, coach."

"Touché," Brian said, "but what exactly should we start teaching them now at this age?"

"Your kids are eight and eleven, correct?" David asked.

"Correct," he said. "I remembered this morning during church that you told me once about the money lessons you teach your boys."

"During church? You weren't paying attention to the sermon?"

"Busted!" Brian laughed. "Seriously, I know Noah and Joseph are six and four, so what could you possibly be teaching them already about money?"

"At their age, we keep it very simple. In my opinion parents can't start too early on this subject. It's so important. We call them 'money lessons.' We take them one lesson at a time, and every so often we add another. Right now we have five. I'm telling you, buddy, it works. I bet our boys understand more about money than most kids two or three times their age. They aren't prodigies or anything. Hailey and I just choose to talk about money and finances a lot in our home."

"Yeah," Brian said, "what are those five money lessons?"

"Remember, these are very basic," David added, "but our discussion about them is always more meaningful. We will add more later, but these are our five current money rules: 1) Hard work equals money, 2) Always tithe, 3) Save some of what you earn, 4) Debt is bad, and 5) Money can actually make more money. I can text them to you later. Will that work?"

"That's perfect," Brian said.

David opened his car door and said, "I don't think these need much explanation, but if you want to talk further, give me a call."

"No," Brian said, "the more simplistic the better. Thanks, buddy. Get some rest, and I'll see you tonight."

Before walking away, Brian waved goodbye to Hailey and the boys.

Chris walked into the already full living room and set the dry-erase board in the corner. "There's not much more space on the board, honey," Chris said to his wife. "You might have to write smaller."

"Oh, just leave the writing up to me," she responded. "If you were in charge of the board, no one would be able to read your scribble."

David opened up in prayer, and they began their sixth week on this parenting topic. "I think we will be able to finish this thing up tonight."

"This has been wonderful," Becca said.

"Well, let's see what God has in store for us tonight," David said. "Jess, Hailey, who wants to share first?"

Hailey motioned toward Jess. "You go ahead. I'm still gathering my thoughts."

"OK, yay, I would love to share," Jess replied in her typical bubbly way. "I want to start by reading a verse." She grabbed her Bible and opened to Matthew 20:28. *The Son of Man did not come to be served, but to serve, and to give his life as a ransom for many.*

"Who was the greatest example of a servant in all of Scripture?" Jess asked.

"Jesus," Hailey answered.

Jess continued, "Thousands of people followed him, including the twelve disciples, who left everything to follow him. So who do you think was the greatest leader in all of Scripture?"

"Jesus, for sure," Hailey answered again.

"Exactly," Jess replied, "and that means Jesus was the greatest servant leader the world has ever known. That's what I think we should add to the board. We should pray that our children become servant leaders."

"I love it," David said enthusiastically.

"Me, too," said Leslie.

"I'm so glad everyone agrees," Jess said. "I really want this one on the final list. Caroline and I talk about this subject a lot. She tends to be a follower and not a leader. At times we should all be followers, especially if we are following godly people, but she sometimes follows the crowd, and that's not leadership."

"Not only is that not leadership, but that can be downright dangerous," David added. "Jess, I love that you attach the word *servant* with leadership. I talk about this with our high-school leaders. There's a book by John Maxwell that I require my student leaders to read *Developing the Leader Within You* by John Maxwell. In the book Maxwell says leadership is influence. It's not a job title or an age or power, and it's certainly not masculine. Leadership is simply having influence over others."

"As parents, we all want our kids to become good leaders, right?" Jess asked. Everyone agreed. "Regardless of their personalities or whether they are extraverted or introverted, we desire for them to be leaders. But I wonder..." She paused. "Are we also teaching our kids to be servants? Think about it—there is so much glory in being the leader. Everyone wants that, right? But there is no glamour in being a servant. It's considered a negative word to some. Yet, Jesus was a servant."

Everyone in the group was taking notes, so no one had a comment or question. Jess had more to say, so she kept talking. "I also wrote this in my notes. Does anyone remember a few months ago when Pastor did that series on leadership?" Everyone nodded. "He gave an analogy that resonated with me, and I definitely think it applies to our discussion about parenting."

"Was it the thing about being a thermostat?" Brian asked.

"Yes, exactly," she answered. "Pastor said Christian leadership is different from much of the world's definitions of leadership. He said Christian leaders should be like thermostats." A few others suddenly remembered his analogy. Realizing that they were catching on, Jess became even more expressive. "A thermometer simply tells you the temperature in a given environment, but it doesn't change or create the temperature. A thermostat literally sets the temperature to whatever degrees you want. As Christian leaders, we want our kids to become thermostats. We pray they will set the spiritual and moral temperature of whatever environment they are in."

"That is influential leadership, because it positively changes others around them," David said. "I love it, Jess. Let's add it to the board."

As Jess stood she said, "One more thing—if we teach our kids to look for ways to serve, more and more opportunities will find them."

"And us," David added. "What a great reminder that we should set a good example for our kids of what it looks like to be servant leaders. I needed that reminder, Jess. Thank you."

"Me, too," Chris admitted.

Jess practically skipped across the room. She was excited. The board was filling up, but she still had room to write, *#12—Servant leaders.*

We Want Our Kids to Become…
#1—Godly young men and women
#2—In love with Jesus and his Word
#3—Respected in their community
#4—Respectful to all people
#5—Humble at all times
#6—Honoring toward women
#7—Full of character and integrity
#8—Hardworking and entrepreneurial
#9—Well-mannered
#10—Submissive to authority
#11—Wise stewards with money
#12—Servant leaders

"How do we know when we are finished?" Brian asked. "How will we recognize when this list is complete?"

Leslie agreed with her husband. "That's a good question. Each time I think the list couldn't get any better, someone adds another trait, and then I think, *Well, I want*

my kids to be good in that area. Is there ever going to be a stop-
ping point?"

"That is a good question," David replied. "In my humble opinion, the purpose of this exercise is not to come
up with one exhaustive list every Christian parent should
adopt and never change. Our goal is to think beyond today
and intentionally raise our kids for tomorrow. The list we
create together is *a* guide, not *the* guide. Even when we all
finish sharing, it still might not be officially complete. We
may choose to add to it later as we gain experience and
knowledge."

"How will we decide when to finish it up, at least for the
time being?" Becca asked.

"Prayer," Hailey said. "Once we all finish sharing what's
on our hearts, we need to bathe it in prayer and ask God to
reveal that answer to us."

David added, "That's exactly right, honey. We all definitely need to give this over to God if anything truly life-
transforming is going to come from it. After all, this isn't
just a sweet little list of good ideas or great qualities. We're
talking about how we are going to definitively and purposefully raise our children. This is a really big deal. We
shouldn't presume to begin this new journey unless we feel
certain God has ordained it."

"Amen!" Jess replied.

"Double amen from me," Brian added.

"Let's further the discussion," David said. "Hailey, I
know you have one to share."

Hailey took the floor. "All our friends and family know
how important this is to David and me," she said. "A top priority in our home is to live with gratitude. This is something

we talk about almost daily, not only with our boys but also as partners. It is so easy to be negative or to complain or to wish we had more or to compare ourselves with someone else. We have to stop sometimes and count our blessings. We talk to the kids routinely about what they are thankful for in life."

"I've heard you guys do that many times," Leslie said. "It's so cool that you remind Noah and Joseph just how blessed you guys are."

"We can always do better, but it certainly is a priority for us," David replied.

"I don't mean to make this about us," Hailey explained. "That's not what I meant, but I think it's extremely important that we all instill within our children a spirit of gratitude. You guys all know about our 'thankful bench' at home. It might sound silly, but I wish every family had a thankful bench. It gives us perspective when we need it. It forces us to stop and be thankful for God's many blessings—the small things as well as the big things in life. David is the best I've ever seen at this. He almost never complains, even when it would be justified. He puts us in check when we are being too negative or complaining or having a bad day."

"Enough about me—let's talk more about me," David joked. Everyone laughed, and then David said, "I learned that from my father. He taught me to have a positive perspective on life."

Hailey found a place in her Bible. "I want to read this real quick," she said. "Everyone knows Philippians 4:13, right? It's one of the most famous verses in the Bible. But it's the previous verse we discuss in our home—Philippians 4:12."

I know what it is to be in need, and I know what it is to have plenty. I have learned the secret of being content in any and every situation, whether well fed or hungry, whether living in plenty or in want.

She continued, "*The secret of being content*—that's what we want for our kids. When times are good, we want them to be grateful for God's blessings and provisions. When times are hard, we want them to be grateful for the opportunity to learn and grow and depend of God."

Everyone was taking notes, except Scott. He was listening but looked kind of zoned out. David asked curiously, "Scott, is something wrong?"

Realizing he was subconsciously wearing his emotions on his face, which he never did, Scott became embarrassed. The others stopped writing and looked up at him. Scott responded by saying nothing was wrong, but he instantly felt convicted by his lie. "I'm sorry. Yes, something is wrong," he admitted. "I stopped because I feel guilty. I didn't realize it was all over my face." He looked at Becca, who was sitting next to him, and then he turned away from her. "I have really failed my family in this area. I know God has blessed our family, but all I do is complain. Almost every day when I come home, I spend thirty minutes talking about everything bad that happened at work. I now realize how negatively that must affect our kids. No one wants to be around that."

Becca didn't say anything. Instead, she grabbed her husband's hand. Scott squeezed her hand and turned to speak to her. "I need to be more grateful and appreciative. If we are going to instill this characteristic in our kids, it must start with me. I need to change."

Becca didn't know exactly how to respond. She wanted to say something or cry or hug him, but she did none of that. Instead she just smiled and stared into her loving husband's eyes. Her look said more than any words could have.

"Thank you for being honest and vulnerable," David said in a soft tone.

It was a special moment that touched everyone in the group. They all new how difficult it was for Scott to confess his struggles in front of everyone. They saw on Becca's face how much she appreciated his vulnerability. God was doing good things. No other words needed to be said, so Jess quietly walked to the dry-erase board. Without asking or commenting, she wrote down, *#13—Grateful, thankful, and content.*

We Want Our Kids to Become...
#1—Godly young men and women
#2—In love with Jesus and his Word
#3—Respected in their community
#4—Respectful to all people
#5—Humble at all times
#6—Honoring toward women
#7—Full of character and integrity
#8—Hardworking and entrepreneurial
#9—Well-mannered
#10—Submissive to authority
#11—Wise stewards with money
#12—Servant leaders
#13—Grateful, thankful, and content

"Oh, I almost forgot—I baked some cookies," Jess suddenly remembered. "Let me grab them real quick. Please don't say anything important while I'm gone."

"Important? Why start now?" Brian said, smiling. Jess went into the kitchen for the cookies, while the others struck up conversations about work and sports. Jess returned carrying a tray of her chocolate chip cookies, fan favorites among the group. No one dared eat more than two, because they were so rich and sweet.

"Delicious!" Brian said, with a mouthful of chocolaty goodness.

"Are you ever going to share your recipe?" It was probably the tenth time Becca had asked over the years, but Jess would never tell her secret.

"If you want these cookies, you have to come over and eat them here," Jess replied. She always gave that same answer to anyone who asked for the recipe. "And you are welcome here anytime. I'm glad you like them."

David swallowed his final bite, licked chocolate from his fingers, and then grabbed his notes. "Thank you, Jess. Those were great as always. OK, guys, let's finish up." Everyone found their seats and looked at David. "I have one more characteristic I would like to share from my list," David said. "Before we wrap this up, does anyone else have one to discuss? Or has everyone already shared all the traits from your personal lists?"

"We don't have any more," Becca said, pointing to Scott.

"No, Brian and I have mentioned all of ours," Leslie agreed.

"We're good, too," said Jess.

"OK, great, maybe we will actually finish this up tonight after all." David smiled. "This has been such an amazing journey."

"We're done after this?" Brian asked.

"I don't know," David admitted. "Let me share this last trait, and then we'll discuss what to do next."

"Sounds good. Whatcha got, buddy?"

"I know that I can be long-winded," David said, "but I will keep this brief and to the point."

Brian put his hand up to his mouth, like he was about to cough, and with a loud voice he coughed the words, "Yeah, right!"

Everyone laughed, and even David was thrown off. "Do you ever stop?" David asked through his own laughter. "What I was about to say before I was so rudely interrupted," he said expressively, "is that I want to read a familiar passage. Open up to Second Chronicles, first chapter, verses ten through twelve. Everyone knows about the wealth of Solomon, but this passage explains how he got it. It starts with Solomon speaking to God."

"Give me wisdom and knowledge, that I may lead this people, for who is able to govern this great people of yours?" God said to Solomon, "Since this is your heart's desire and you have not asked for wealth, possessions or honor, nor for the death of your enemies, and since you have not asked for a long life but for wisdom and knowledge to govern my people over whom I have made you king, therefore wisdom and knowledge will be given you. And I will also give you wealth, possessions and honor, such as no king who was before you ever had and none after you will have."

When David finished reading, he looked up at his friends and said, "When God told Solomon he would give him whatever he asked for, Solomon asked for two things: wisdom and discernment. This is my prayer for myself almost every day of my life for the last twenty years. My father taught me how to pray and ask God for wisdom and discernment, and that's exactly what I desire for my boys. I don't know of anything more valuable to a Christian man or woman than to be filled with wisdom and discernment. I hope my kids become smart and educated in school, but I would much rather them become wise. I hope they have great athletic ability, but I would much prefer them to have discernment."

Everyone in the group listened intently. Because they were all friends, the group enjoyed joking and cutting up. But they knew how to get serious when it was time, and they respected David so much. Everyone in the group, whether as a couple or individually, had many times privately sought David's advice, counsel, or help. He was far from perfect, but when it came to helping people through difficult or confusing situations, the Holy Spirit clearly spoke through him. When David said he had been praying twenty years for God to fill him with the wisdom and discernment of Solomon, everyone was intrigued.

"Nothing is more difficult than parenting," he continued, "and nothing is more important either. I recommend two things. First, pray daily that God would give us the wisdom to raise our kids to become godly young men and women. Or, as Solomon says in verse ten, *'wisdom and knowledge to lead and govern this people.'* My second recommendation is to teach our children how and why to pray for God's wisdom and discernment for their lives.

When our children pray for wisdom, you watch and see what will happen," David leaned up on the edge of his chair. "Friends, classmates, teammates, and even adults will seek them out for help. People will sense it and see it in their lives. Many are smart, athletic, and talented, but I wonder how many seek wisdom and discernment? One of my favorite Proverbs is chapter twenty, verse fifteen. It says, '*Gold there is, and rubies in abundance, but lips that speak knowledge are a rare jewel.*'" With his best Forrest Gump impression, David concluded, "And that's all I have to say about that."

Everyone quietly processed David's words. Brian broke the silence. "I owe you an apology. You actually were brief and to the point. That must be a new record for you." David smiled at his friend, but this time no one laughed. Brian changed his tone and added, "But seriously, that's good stuff. It seems overwhelming to teach my kids wisdom when I probably don't have it myself."

David corrected him. "I didn't say we should have wisdom or teach wisdom. I said we should pray for God to give us wisdom as parents and then teach our children how to pray for it also. I certainly don't always have wisdom, but I do ask God for it. Does that make sense?" David looked at Brian, but he intended the question for everyone.

"It makes complete sense," Hailey answered on behalf of the group.

David looked at his watch. It was 7:40 p.m. "I'm sorry, guys. We have gone over tonight," he said. "Jess, please write this down so we can get out of your hair."

"Absolutely!" She jumped up. "Last but not least, great one to end on." With no room at the bottom of the columns, she had to write sideways, but there was barely space for her to squeeze in *#14—Wise and discerning.*

We Want Our Kids to Become...
#1—Godly young men and women
#2—In love with Jesus and his Word
#3—Respected in their community
#4—Respectful to all people
#5—Humble at all times
#6—Honoring toward women
#7—Full of character and integrity
#8—Hardworking and entrepreneurial
#9—Well-mannered
#10—Submissive to authority
#11—Wise stewards with money
#12—Servant leaders
#13—Grateful, thankful, and content
#14—Wise and discerning

Jess sat back down, and everyone looked at the dry-erase board. It was completely full from top to bottom. Six weeks of prayer, reflection, study, and discussion, and this was the outcome. It looked daunting and overwhelming, but at the same time simple and exciting. These were more than just words and phrases. This board represented their children and the future they desired for them. It was only a cheap dry-erase board with markers, and yet it was beautiful.

"What now?" Chris asked.

"When I look at that list, I don't know if I should feel prepared or intimidated," Brian said. "To be honest, I'm feeling kind of both."

Leslie nodded and said, "No kidding."

"Are we finished? Is there anything else to add?" Hailey asked the group. No one knew how to respond, so no one did.

David once again allowed for awkward silence. He enjoyed listening to his friends think out loud and then discussing their feelings. A healthy spirit of awe, confusion, and excitement was in the room. Everyone knew they were part of something special. Something really big was going to happen in their families, but no one knew exactly what to do next. Finally, Scott looked at the group leader and asked, "What do we do now, David?"

David confessed with complete transparency, "I don't really know for sure. I'll tell you what my gut says. I don't think we should make any rash conclusions or emotional decisions tonight. Instead, we'll all agree to pray about it for one week. Everyone write down these fourteen characteristics and traits, and take them home with you. Let's make a pact to commit them to prayer every day this week. Ask God, 'Is this list complete?' Ask him if this parenting standard is biblical and from the Lord." David walked over to the board and pointed at the list. "Perhaps most important, are these the type of men and women we want to raise?"

Hailey picked up where her husband left off. "After all of us pray about it this week, we can come back next Sunday and make a decision. If we all feel at peace about it, we can adopt this standard into our own families."

"Exactly," David concluded. "In the meantime, I'll close us out in prayer tonight." They all bowed their heads as he prayed:

"Father, we are so thankful for this time together, to be able to walk in true biblical community with like-minded believers. Father, we need you now. We have a major task in front of us and need your guidance. Holy Spirit, as we all seek you this week, will you please speak to us individually as well as collectively? Clear our minds and hearts so you can teach us. Father, we desire more than anything to be great parents, but we admit we are nothing without you. We desire to raise our children to become godly adults, but we acknowledge we need the guidance of the Holy Spirit living in us. Please give us the answers we seek and the courage to live it out. We are your open vessels. In the name of Jesus, I pray. Amen."

CHAPTER THIRTEEN

I t was Saturday night, and David was tucking Noah and Joseph into bed. Hailey had already said good night to the kids, and now David was going through his nightly routine. Bedtime was his favorite part of the day. Sometimes the mundane routine of going through the bedtime motions could be exhausting, but he loved the final few minutes he got to spend with his boys. "Is there anything you want to talk about?" he asked Noah.

"No, sir," Noah replied.

"Are you sure? Anything happen at school that maybe you don't understand or you need me to explain? Have you seen or heard anything lately that upset or confused you?"

"No, sir, nothing tonight," Noah repeated.

"OK, well, you can always talk to me or your mother about anything. You know that, right?"

"Yes, sir."

"Hey, you had a great game today." David stroked Noah's hair.

"But I got out twice," Noah argued.

"I know, but that's baseball," David said. "Even the best players in the world get out. You hustled on every play, I heard you use great manners with your coach, and you were the first player in line to shake the other team's hands when you lost. I'm proud of you, buddy. You are a good kid."

"Thanks, Daddy."

"All right, get some sleep. We have church in the morning." David kissed him on the forehead. "Can I tell you three things?"

"I know, Dad," Noah smiled. "'You're special. God loves you. And Daddy loves you.'"

David had repeated these words hundreds of times, but he had heard them thousands of times before. These were the same three phrases his father told him every day of his childhood. In fact, they were the last words his father spoke to him through his final letter before his death. Now David shared the words with his boys every night since they were born. David smiled back at his precious boy. "Good night, buddy."

"Good night, Daddy."

David turned off the lights and went into Joseph's room to carry out the same routine slightly modified for a four-year-old. After he said good night to Joseph, he walked down the hall to his bedroom. Hailey was in bed, playing on her phone.

"What are doing over there?" he asked his wife. "Watching a silly cat video on Facebook or something?" He laughed at his own joke and went into the bathroom to brush his teeth.

Hailey didn't acknowledge his sarcasm but answered, "I'm texting back and forth with Jess, Becca, and Leslie."

From the bathroom, David shouted, "The four of you are in a group text together? That could go on all night."

"Ha-ha, you're so funny," Hailey replied with her own tone of sarcasm.

David walked out of the bathroom with his toothbrush in his mouth. "What are you ladies talking about?" he asked. Even though he enjoyed joking with his wife, he appreciated so much that she enjoyed keeping up with the ladies from the group throughout the week. This was not David's strength, so he valued it in her. He was more of a teacher, and she was the relationship person. They each had their own set of gifts, but together they were a complete team. After a decade and a half of marriage and ministry, they had learned how to utilize their strengths and complement each other's weaknesses.

Hailey answered, "I was asking them how they did this week in praying over our parenting list, but then we got into all the things we've been talking about in our group for the last several weeks. They are so excited."

David stood in the doorway, beaming with pride. It excited him when people he loved were learning, growing, and changing. With toothpaste foaming at his mouth, he was barely able to utter an audible word. "Like what?"

Hailey stopped texting and looked up at her husband. She laughed and said, "You know you've got toothpaste all over your face, right?" David kept brushing, and she continued. "We were all sharing a few things we have already begun implementing with our kids. This is so neat, David. I can't believe how much impact this parenting class is having on everyone. This is real-life change. You'll love it because it's all simple, practical stuff they are sharing—just like that conversation you and I had after the parenting conference in Lexington."

David rushed into the bathroom and spit into the sink. He shouted, "I'd love to hear all about it." He rinsed out his mouth and then, literally, *jumped* into bed.

"David, don't do that. You're going to break the bed." Hailey's voice was raised.

"Tell me all about it," he said.

"Hold on." Hailey went back and read all the texts to David. They spent the next hour reading text messages and talking about their small group. God truly was at work in these families. What they didn't know was that this was only the beginning.

It was 6:35 p.m. on Sunday night, and the group was already thirty minutes into their meeting. David asked the ladies to share some of the stories they had texted about the night before. It was powerful and emotional to listen to stories from these great parents, who now had even more purpose and strategy for raising the children they loved so deeply. They were the exact same people they were six weeks before, but listening to them talk, it was obvious they now felt more prepared and equipped.

"Thank you, everyone, for sharing those stories," David said, trying to switch gears. "It gives me much joy to hear what God is doing in our families. I know I say this all of the time, but this is what a church small group is all about. It's about doing real life together with like-minded believers and living in true biblical community."

"Amen," Becca quietly whispered.

David continued, "When we left here last week, we all agreed to pray fervently about whether or not our parenting standard is complete. We could add to it later, but is this list of fourteen qualities and character traits where we want to begin? Before we move forward, does anyone want to add anything, take anything away, or make a comment?"

"Just like you guys, I prayed about this all week," Brian answered, unusually serious. "I even fasted during one of my lunches at school. I had never fasted before, and, boy, was I hungry," he said with a half smile. "I also have never been so close to God. I've heard Christians talk about peace before, but I honestly don't think I ever fully understood what that meant until this week." Brian was definitely speaking from the heart. "Now I can say without question that I have peace about this parenting standard."

"I'm proud of you, buddy," David said to his friend.

"I agree with Brian," Jess added. "Not only am I excited about this, but I truly feel I am going to be a better mother moving forward." Jess began to tear up, but that was normal. In the past, she easily cried about almost anything. Usually it made everyone laugh, including Jess, but no one laughed this time.

"Scott and I want to adopt this list with our children," Becca agreed. "We talked about it several times this week, and there is nothing we want to change at this point."

"I think we're all on board," Hailey concluded, looking to her husband.

Back to his regular self, Brian suggested they seal the deal by cutting their hands, shaking on it, and becoming blood brothers. Everyone, of course, laughed uncontrollably.

"As great as that sounds, Brian, I have a less painful idea," David responded. "There is no right or wrong way to do this, nor is there a biblical mandate. But now that we've all prayed about it and agreed on this list, here is what I suggest we do. Each couple should sit down with their kids and go over this list together. Be honest and transparent with them. Tell them what's going on and what we have been discussing and learning in small group."

"I already typed up the list and printed it off for Noah and Joseph," Hailey said to the group. "We haven't gone over it with the boys yet, but I am going to have them hang it in their rooms. Not that you guys should do that, but I just want to share what we are doing."

"Yeah, great idea," Leslie responded.

"I think I will do that too," Becca agreed. "That way they have it to look at it and be constantly reminded of what we hope to accomplish as parents."

"That's exactly what I was thinking," Hailey replied.

"Just tell them what we've been discussing and then read it to them?" Scott asked.

"Well, everyone is free to handle it however they want," David answered, "but I think if we all play our cards right, this could turn out to be a truly special moment. Sometimes as parents we are afraid to admit our weaknesses to our kids. We don't want them to see that we don't always know what we're doing and don't have it all figured out, right?" Everyone agreed. "I am guilty of that too," he said. "How cool would it be—no, change that to how *powerful* would it be if we started by admitting we don't have it all figured out? We tell them we desire to raise them into godly young men and women, but that we can't do it alone. We need the help and guidance of the Holy Spirit, God's Word, and like-minded believers. When we go over the list with them, what we are saying is that we now have a biblical strategy. We know exactly the kind of men and women we want to raise. But here's where the moment could turn crazy awesome—using this list as our new standard, we might need to apologize for some things. We might need to admit to some weaknesses and pray about it with them. We might even need to ask forgiveness from our kids for some things we've done or areas in which we have fallen short. And we might need to explain how and why some things are going to change moving forward."

This was a radical thought that seemed to catch everyone off guard. Feeling sensitive to the moment, Hailey spoke. "David and I stayed up for over an hour last night, talking about this. My initial response was that it seemed a bit overwhelming. But the more we talked about it, I started thinking perhaps this is exactly how God wants it. Our kids don't need us to be perfect. They just need as to be parents. Maybe God wants us to be vulnerable and honest with them. Instead of seeing this as a new list of rules, our kids can see it for what it is—a biblical strategy to help them mature."

"I'm glad you explained that," Scott replied. "When I was thinking and praying about it, I never even considered exactly how Becca and I would start implementing this new parenting idea. I wasn't planning to sit down with them and go over it. I just figured we would do some things differently, but it makes sense to include them in the process."

Hailey quickly responded, "That's actually something we discussed last night, Scott. The reason we are including our boys in this process is that we want to be on the same page with them. We want them to understand why we do certain things as parents."

"Or why you *don't* do certain things other families do," Jess added.

"Yes, exactly," Hailey agreed. "Isn't that the truth? There are many things David and I choose not to do with or for our boys that other parents may think is great. That's the power of having this list. Whenever a situation arises or a decision needs to made, we have a guide to help us."

"I prefer the word 'standard,' but that's exactly right," David said. "I think everyone will agree that many options in life aren't necessarily good or bad...or issues of right or wrong. During these situations, we simply make decisions as parents that are in the best interests of our children and our families. We decide what's most important to us, right?"

"I'm following you," Chris replied.

"I'm glad at least one person is," David joked. "It's in these moments that I think good parents become great parents. Almost all Christian parents know what to do when dealing with issues of sin or morality. But when it comes to everyday scenarios, we need to win as parents. It is in these real-life, common situations that our new parenting standard will help us most."

Brian put his hands up to his head, making sounds and motions like bombs were exploding in his brain. "Dude, this whole time we've been discussing this issue, I never thought about it like that. In my head I've been envisioning this list to help Leslie and me with bigger decisions about our kids—really important issues and stuff like that. I wasn't thinking about everyday situations."

Chris looked at Brian and said, "I was getting ready to say the same thing."

David suddenly felt that perhaps he hadn't been communicating well. After all, he had wrestled with these thoughts for many months now, but it was still new and fresh to the others. He knew everyone was in agreement about the value of the list of traits they had created. However, they needed to also fully understand the reason behind it in order to make significant impacts in their families. He looked up at the dry-erase board and then back down at his notes. On top of his notes was a printed list of the fourteen characteristics. Above the list were these words: *We Want Our Kids to Become...*

David grabbed the paper and held it up high. "From this day forward, everything we do as parents is for this outcome in our children," he said. "This is our plan, our strategy, our new standard. Every parenting decision we make, big or small, is to accomplish this," he pointed to the paper, which he still held high. "Every rule we establish in our homes, every creative idea we think of, and even the events we choose to put on our calendars—it all has a purpose now."

All eyes in the room were locked on David. He was always a passionate man, but he now spoke with an intensity he hadn't shown before. Several months of combined contemplation, personal reflection, and prayer poured from his mouth. "No more random parenting," he continued. "No more trying to figure it all out as we go. No more simply hoping our kids turn out well one day. There is a better way. Now we know to the best of our ability—and even our kids will know—exactly the kind of men and women who we seek to raise. We won't be perfect parents, and they won't be perfect children, but at least everyone in the family will understand the ultimate destination."

This was more than a speech—David was issuing a challenge, perhaps the most important challenge of their lives. Everyone sensed the gravity of the situation. It was as if six weeks of discussion and prayer had for the first time become real to the group. Leslie thought, *Two years of being in this small group, and it all comes down to this moment. God not only brought us to these people, but he brought us to this moment. Now we have to decide what type of parents we will become.*

Brian spoke up. "This might sound like a vague question, but what's next? What do we do now?"

David replied, "Teach and model." Brian stared at David, waiting for him to say more. "That's it," David eventually said. "We teach and model."

"Teach and model what exactly?" Brian asked.

"This list," David replied, holding up his paper. "Ultimately we can't *make* our children turn out a certain way. We can't force them to learn this stuff." He again pointed to the list. "But here's what I know to be the gospel truth. This is one thing we can control, a standard for what we as parents can do." David engaged the others. "We can make ourselves teach and model these qualities and traits. Every parent I know has a strong desire to be a good mother or father, but being a good parent is absolutely not our objective. My goal is not to be good father. Sounds weird, right?"

Already knowing what he was going to say, Hailey indulged him by saying, "Yes, it does."

"My goal is to teach and model this list to my boys," he continued. "That's all I can do, all I *should* do." David stood, walked over to the board, and starting from the top, ticked each item on the list one by one. "Hailey and I have to do this together, but again, I'm going to speak for myself for the moment. My job is to teach Noah and Joseph what it looks like to be a godly man.

"My job is to model to them what it looks like to love Jesus and the Word of God.

"To model for them how to be respected in our community.

"To teach them to also be respectful to all people.

"To model humility.

"To teach them how to honor their mother and all women.

"To model character and integrity for them in public and in private.

"To teach them to work hard and become entrepreneurial.

"To teach them manners and why we use them.

"To model submission to the authorities in my life.

"To model good stewardship of our family finances and resources.

"To teach them how to be servant leaders.

"To teach them to be grateful and thankful in all circumstances.

"And finally, my goal is to model wisdom and discernment in my own life."

CHAPTER FOURTEEN

It was a beautiful Thursday afternoon in Louisville. Hailey, returning from the grocery store, pulled into her neighborhood. The trees and flowers were in full bloom, and the sky was clear blue. She loved nature and often felt closest to God while outdoors. As she drove toward her home, she prayed silently as she did almost every day. It was her normal routine to prepare her mind and heart before she walked in the door to see her family. This was a practice David had taught her years ago, a practice he had learned from his father. "Don't take your stresses and worries home with you," David's father used to tell him. "Give those over to God before you walk in the door. Your kids deserve your best, not your leftovers."

For the last several years, Hailey had applied this spiritual practice in her life. She sometimes forgot, of course, but she was usually consistent. The undeniable reality was that she could tell a difference in her attitude and personality on the days she prayed versus the days she forgot. So almost every day when she pulled into her neighborhood, she said a quick prayer. Some days, she asked God to remove her stress or fears. Other days, she simply thanked God for his many blessings or for the health of their children. Either way, by the time she said "amen" in the driveway, she was prepared mentally, emotionally, and spiritually to walk in the door and be the best wife and mother possible.

This day was no exception. As she smiled and waved to her neighbors who were outside, she whispered a short prayer from her heart as she neared her driveway.

> "Lord Jesus, thank you for this beautiful day, which you have created. When I look at the sky and trees and flowers, I see just a glimpse of your goodness. Thank you, Jesus, for allowing us to live in this home. Thank you for the money to buy these groceries. Help me to never take for granted the blessings you give us. Please prepare my heart and mind to be present and focused on my family. Help me, Lord, to love and serve my husband and kids with kindness and joy. For your glory, amen."

As soon as she finished her prayer, Hailey pulled in and saw Noah's bicycle blocking her path in the middle of the garage. She had told him a thousand times not to leave his bike out. She'd warned him over and over that one day she might accidentally run it over. Normally frustrated by this occurrence, on this day she laughed. She knew that if she hadn't just finished praying, she would be completely annoyed. She probably would have walked in the house and fussed at her son. She would have felt justified, but to what avail? Instead she calmly put her car in park, got out, and moved his bike to where it belonged. She said out loud, "Lord, I didn't know I would need you so quickly."

Hailey went inside to ask her boys for help unloading the groceries, but she saw that David was standing in the hallway and having what appeared to be a serious conversation with Noah. She didn't want to interrupt, so she just listened and waited. David's arm was wrapped around his six-year-old son. They both looked at the large picture, which had hung on their wall for almost two years. Hailey instantly knew what David was doing, because he had done it many times before.

"Son, it means something to be in this family," she heard him say. "We are not perfect, nor are we better than anyone else, but it still means something very special to be in this family." Noah looked straight ahead at the picture and listened to a message he had heard from his dad many times before. David looked down at his son and continued. "Your name means something, too. Your last name, our family name, says something about you. Did you know that?"

"Yes, sir," Noah answered, still looking at the picture on the wall.

"Not only that, but your last name also says something about me, your mother, and the grandfather you never got to meet. To be in the Williams family, we all need to live by certain expectations." Noah knew what his dad was about to say, but he listened respectfully. "Look at this, Noah," David said, pointing to the large picture. "These are not just a bunch of meaningless words and Bible verses. This represents who we are and how we live. This is what it means to be in the Williams family. We live a certain way. We act a certain way. We love a certain way. We treat people a certain way. We talk a certain way. We even dress a certain way."

"I know, Daddy," Noah replied.

David squeezed his son tightly and then kissed him on the head. It wasn't until he turned and looked at Hailey that she realized Noah wasn't in trouble. Usually when David talked about what it means to be in the Williams family, it meant one of the boys had done something wrong or unwise, and he was using it as a teachable moment. But every once in a while, he just stood with the kids, looked at the picture, and read it together for no other reason than the fact that he loved his boys. Hailey smiled. "Hey, guys."

"Hey, little lady," David said. "Do you need help?"

"Yes, that would be great. I'm exhausted," she replied.

David said, "Boys, let's help Mommy put the groceries away, please." Two small sets of hands and feet headed for the car to bring in the food.

An hour later, the Williams family was sitting around the kitchen table for dinner. Family dinner was a high priority. There was no TV, no cell phones, and no video games—just good old-fashioned conversation. With the busyness of life, it was sometimes challenging to sit down together for dinner. But Hailey and David had decided years ago that it would remain a top priority to carve out thirty minutes each evening to enjoy dinner as a family. Of course, many nights there were scheduling conflicts. But though they had work, school activities, church, and sports, they did their best to create this moment as frequently as possible, even when it meant saying no to other opportunities.

After several minutes of going around the table so everyone could share about his or her day, Hailey looked at David and said, "I've been thinking about something."

"You, thinking? That's awfully dangerous," he joked. The boys laughed.

Being the only female in the family, Hailey normally took the brunt of the jokes. She knew the boys were only kidding around and that they all loved her very much, so she didn't mind. "You need some new material," she said with a smirk.

"What have you been thinking about?" David asked.

"About the small group and what to do next," she replied.

"Oh really? What do you think we should do now that we're finished with parenting?"

"Actually, I don't think we're done quite yet."

"OK," David answered, curious, "but we've been discussing biblical parenting for two months. Everyone is on the same page about being purposeful and intentional with their kids. So what else can we talk about?"

Hailey pointed over his shoulders. "I think you should talk about that," she said. David turned and looked at the large picture on the wall. "It hit me hard when I came in and saw you talking with Noah," Hailey said. "It was the craziest thing." Hailey looked as if a light bulb had suddenly come on in her mind. "You talk to the boys about that so often, but I have never thought about it like this before."

David asked, "Thought about it like how?"

"Like what it can do for others," she replied. "I love what it means, but honestly, I've always just thought about it from the standpoint of our family and our kids. I've never thought about how much it could benefit other families, have you?"

David set his fork down. He was puzzled. The guy who was known for thinking of everything had never thought about this before. "I guess not," he said softly.

"When I listened to you and Noah earlier, I felt like God was speaking to me. Not in an audible voice, of course, but it felt as if he was telling me you need to share this with others. This is a very special thing you do with the boys. You need to share it with others. Maybe you should preach about it or teach it to the student ministry parents, but I definitely believe you are supposed to teach it to the small group." Hailey was not normally a very serious person, but she spoke with a rare tone of strength and authority.

David respected his wife, and he certainly respected the role of the Holy Spirit in her life. Many times over the years, God gave her a strong conviction about something or someone, and she almost always turned out to be right or justified in her instinct. Hailey was a prayer warrior, but very seldom did she say God was telling her to do something unless she truly believed it. David took her words seriously. "*Supposed* to?" David asked. "That's a strong word. Why do you think I'm supposed to teach it?"

"I stood watching you share what it means to be in our family, and all I could think about were Scott and Becca, Brian and Leslie, and Chris and Jess. Something in my gut said that they need this, that they would benefit from this, that it would add value to their families." She paused, searching for her words. "Right before I got home from the grocery store, I was in deep prayer with the Lord. I did a lot of talking but had not listened to him. When I walked in the house and saw you guys, it was God responding back to me, telling me to stop and listen. I don't say this lightly, David, but God wants you to teach this stuff to our small group."

"Did God talk to you, Mommy?" Noah asked. He was very inquisitive and perceptive for his age. David and Hailey had to be very careful when talking because he seemed to pick up on everything even when they didn't think he was listening.

Hailey smiled at her son. "I think so, honey, but not in actual words like we are using. It was more of a feeling I had. God was talking to my heart."

"About what it means to be a Williams?" he asked.

"Yes."

Noah turned to David. "Are you going to teach others about what we do, Daddy?"

"I don't know, buddy. What do you think I should do?" David asked his six-year-old son.

"Hmmm…" Noah tried to think of an answer. "Would it help other families be like ours?"

"Not like ours," David explained. "No one needs to be like us, but Mommy is saying it might help others have stronger families."

"Then yes," he said with a smile, as if he had just solved a puzzle. "I think you should. If others can have a strong family like ours, then why wouldn't you help them?"

David looked up at Hailey, who tried to hold back her laughter.

"May I please be excused?" Noah asked.

Smiling through her teeth, Hailey replied, "Yes, you can, honey, but clean up your plate first."

Following his big brother's lead, Joseph asked and was granted the same. The boys threw their napkins into the trash, put their plates and cups in the dishwasher, and then headed for the playroom. After they left the room, Hailey turned to David and said, "He's your son!"

"He is so funny, isn't he?" David replied.

"So what do you think, David? Why do you seem hesitant?" she asked.

"I'm not hesitant. I agree with you that it's a good idea," he answered. "My only concern is that I don't want to come across the wrong way. I don't want to give off the false perception that we are these amazing parents or that we have it all figured out."

"I totally agree with you. I was thinking the same thing while cooking dinner. They all know we aren't a perfect family. They know us—warts and all. We have shared some of our weaknesses and issues with Noah in the past. I keep coming back to one question. If you hadn't come up with this, wouldn't you want someone to share it with you? Think about how much value it has added to us as parents."

David thought for a second and said, "Yes, if someone I trusted were to share this with me, I would be very grateful. But don't you think it's too personal? Coming up with our parenting standard as a group is one thing because it applies to everyone, but this is very private. The title is 'What does it mean to be a Williams?'"

"Yes, but it can be tweaked for each family," she replied. "It's not about our family; it's about the message. Trust me—they would want to know about this and use it with their own children."

"Can we have group here?" David asked.

"Here?" Hailey responded. "I would love to host everyone, but why?"

"First, because I think Brian is the only one in the group who has ever been here. The Clines' house is so large and perfect for what we do, so I definitely want to keep meeting there in the future. It's still kind of sad that we have never had everyone over here before. We need to do that as leaders."

"I would love that," she said.

"More than that, if I am going to teach about this, I want them here so I can show them what we do and how we do it. It will probably only take one or two weeks to get it done, but I think doing it here will be best."

"Sounds good. Are you wanting to show them the picture?" Hailey asked.

"Just briefly, but yes," he answered.

"OK, I'll send out a group text and tell everyone we will meet here for the next week or two." Hailey got up to wash the dishes. She said under her breath but loud enough for him to hear, "Or three or four, knowing you."

David said nothing, but he smirked and raised his eyebrows.

CHAPTER FIFTEEN

"Look who is the last to arrive," David said to Brian, inviting him and Leslie into his home.

Brian gave his buddy a hug. "I told Leslie, on the way over here, the only reason we're having group at your house tonight is so you won't be the last to show up for a change."

David talked with Leslie, and their kids took off to the playroom, where the other children were waiting. "Your home is beautiful," Leslie said.

"Thank you," David replied. "Brian has been here a couple times, but I can't believe you haven't." When Brian and Leslie joined the group nearly two years before, they were having marital problems, which stemmed from the fact that Brian was not yet a believer at the time. He had been to the Williams' house alone a few times to meet with David for counseling and help.

David, Brian, and Leslie walked into the living room, where the others were already sitting and talking. Scott said, "Brian, congratulations on winning the season opener on Friday. I took the kids to the game, and we had a blast."

"Oh, I didn't know you were there. Thanks for coming out to support us," Brian said. "I have tunnel vision during the games, so I never know who is in the stands. I don't even say hello to my own mother."

"Defending state champs!" Hailey said excitedly. "Are we going back to back?"

"That's the goal," Brian affirmed. "Most of our starters are back, and our pitching should be better than last season. If the boys stay focused and don't walk around with big heads, we'll be tough to beat."

Leslie put her hand on her husband's leg and said, "OK, OK, we better change the subject before he really gets revved up. He could easily talk about baseball the entire hour."

Brian shrugged. "What? I thought everyone came to hear me talk about baseball."

"Actually, we came to listen to David," Leslie retorted.

"You guys are hilarious," David laughed.

"I am excited to hear about what we're doing tonight," Jess added. "Chris and I were just saying the other day how sad we were that our parenting discussion was over. When I got the text from Hailey, I was pumped." Jess turned to Hailey. "Your text was so vague, though, so Chris and I are very curious about what we're going to learn tonight."

"Yeah, sorry," Hailey apologized. "I was going to be more specific, but it's impossible to explain in a text. David can talk about it better than I can. I'm sorry for the last-minute change of venue, but we really appreciate you guys coming here."

"No problem. It was one less day of cleaning for me, so I'm grateful," Jess said, grinning as usual. She had such a pleasing personality.

"Let's get down to business, shall we?" David asked rhetorically. "I want to first say a couple things up front. Hailey told me you guys already know this, but I'll feel much better if I say it anyway. While I am truly passionate about what I want to share with you, it is very important that you know I don't think I'm superior. We are not perfect parents, and we most definitely don't have it all figured out. We still have our struggles from time to time."

Becca said, "Hailey is right, David, you don't have to say that."

"I know, I know," he said. "I just don't want to come across the wrong way. I also know that if I can share some valuable things with you that we do with our boys, then maybe God can use it for good."

"Noah and Joseph are incredible boys, even as young as they are," Becca chimed in. "Anything you want to share about what you do with them, Scott and I are all ears." Scott nodded in agreement.

"Thank you," Hailey said humbly.

"Yes, thank you, Becca," David added. "Here is the last thing I'll say before we get started. As you all know, normally in our small group we have lots of discussion so we can all learn from one another. Even though I teach some, I never want to be a talking head in this group. We are *all* teachers. Just like we did when we created the parenting standard, everyone contributed. I want to apologize in advance for talking and teaching too much. Hailey asked me to teach this, and I don't know any other way to do it."

"David, quit being apologetic," Brian said. "As much as I like to mess around with you, I wouldn't be who I am today if not for your influence. You are a gifted teacher, so teach."

It was exactly what David needed to hear. He was never shy about teaching or leading, but in this group he tried to remain more of a facilitator on purpose. His goal was not to *be* the leader but to *raise* leaders. But he enjoyed teaching, and he had something valuable to share, so he greatly appreciated their encouragement. "Thank you, Brian" he said humbly. "Open your Bibles to Judges, chapter thirteen, please. We all know the story of Samson and his incredible strength."

"And his long hair." Chris rubbed his own bald head.

"Exactly," David said. "I'm not going to teach on Samson, but I want to introduce a thought to you about him that relates to our own families. I'm reading verses two through five."

A certain man of Zorah, named Manoah, from the clan of the Danites, had a wife who was childless, unable to give birth. The angel of the Lord appeared to her and said, "You are barren and childless, but you are going to become pregnant and give birth to a son. Now see to it that you drink no wine or other fermented drink and that you do not eat anything unclean. You will become pregnant and have a son whose head is never to be touched by a razor because the boy is to be a Nazirite, dedicated to God from the womb. He will take the lead in delivering Israel from the hands of the Philistines.

"How in the world does that passage apply to my family?" Brian asked.

"In Scripture, a Nazirite was a person set apart for the work of the Lord. Sometimes a man or woman took a vow to become a Nazirite, and sometimes God instructed certain parents to raise their child with the Nazirite vow. This was the case with Samson, as well as John the Baptist. But follow me on this, because here's my point. For Samson, it meant something very special to be a Nazirite. He had to live by very specific expectations and instructions. Even as a baby and later as a child, the angel of the Lord told Samson's parents, 'God has a purpose and plan for this life; therefore, he will live and act a certain way because he is in the family of God.'" David closed his Bible.

"I'm following you, but can you elaborate a bit more?" Jess asked.

"Everyone, come with me." David stood to his feet. "We are all visual learners, so I want to show you something that will make sense of it all. This is the reason I wanted to have group here tonight."

David led them through the kitchen and into a hallway. He stopped next to a large picture hanging on the wall. It was a tight squeeze, but all eight were jammed in the hallway, not exactly sure what they were doing. David pointed to the picture. "This is why Hailey invited you tonight. This is what she has asked me to share with you." It was a large picture, at least three feet tall and two feet wide. It was filled with words and Bible verses from top to bottom. At the heading of the picture, in large capital letters, were these words: *WHAT DOES IT MEAN TO BE A WILLIAMS?*

After several seconds of reading, Jess softly said, "This is so beautiful."

"Yes, this is priceless," Leslie added.

"Where did you get this?" Chris asked. "Did you come up with this yourself?"

David replied, "We can go back into the living room now, but I wanted you to see this for a reason. I will explain more about it later and tell you what it is and how Hailey and I use it."

"I want to take a picture real quick so I can read it again and look up those Bible verses." Scott took his phone from his pocket.

Before he could open his camera app, Hailey replied, "No need, Scott. I already made copies for everyone. I'll hand them out when we sit back down." After everyone walked back to the living room, Hailey passed around bottles of water. Then she took a stack of papers from her Bible and gave one to each person.

When Chris got his copy, he looked over at David and said, "Seriously, David, did you come up with this? It's incredible."

"Thanks, Chris," he answered. "Yes, Hailey and I came up with this and have been using it with the boys for almost two years."

Hailey spoke up. "'Hailey and I'? No, David wrote this. I read it, but that's about the extent of my involvement."

"No, you helped me finalize it, and we prayed about it together," David said in support of his wife.

As everyone read their copies, David said, "Please feel free to keep reading those, but I promise we will go in depth about everything on it. Before we can get there, I must introduce the concept that got me started down this path two years ago." David turned to Scott and asked, "Will you please read the first verse of chapter twenty-two, Proverbs?"

"Sure." Scott grabbed his Bible and opened up to the middle.

A good name is more desirable than great riches; to be esteemed is better than silver or gold.

David looked around, trying to make eye contact with everyone. "You know how you can read something a thousand times before, and then you read it again and suddenly it speaks to you? Well, that's what happened to me with this verse. I was reading it in my quiet time one day, when all of a sudden it stopped me midsentence. I am money-motivated, as you guys know, so I thought, *Why is my name more important than riches?* I knew Solomon was talking about the importance of a good Christian reputation, but then I thought, *What does my name even mean?*"

David paused, trying to engage his friends. "Seriously, what does 'David Williams' mean? I had never in my life thought of that before. I knew I wanted to have a good reputation in my church and community, but I'm talking about much more than that." David's passion swelled up from within. "This was the moment I asked myself and my Creator, *Who am I? And what name has my father passed down to me?*" As if at the push of a button, David's eyes teared up at the very mention of his father. He immediately laughed, wiping the newly formed tears from his eyes. "Dang it— there I go again," he said aloud through his laughter. "Every time I mention Dad."

Hailey reached over and grabbed his hand.

David quickly regained composure. "Let me take you down the rabbit hole of how I got from there to here." He held up his copy of the paper. "I started thinking about this truth: in the Bible and in biblical times, names meant something. For instance, the name Daniel means 'judgment of God.' Daniel delivered many of God's judgments through his visions and dreams. Do you know the name Joshua means 'deliverer'? That's exactly what Joshua did— he delivered the Israelites into the Promised Land. And here's one more you will all know. This one is cool, because God literally changed his name to mean something specific."

"Peter!" Brian shouted.

"Yep, exactly. God changed Simon's name to Peter, which means 'rock.' God had a plan to establish the church through Simon, but he changed his name to get his attention. God told Peter, 'Your name now means something very special, and I will make you known by it for my glory.' At least, that's my interpretation."

"Did you look up what Williams means?" Brian asked.

"No, I don't really care how Google defines my last name, and I'm not really concerned with its origin," David explained. "That's not what I'm trying to say. My focus isn't on how others define my name. It's on what my name really means right here." He held his hand over his heart. "About two years ago..." He stopped and looked at Hailey. "Wait, has it been that long?"

"Not quite, but almost," she affirmed.

"Almost two years ago, I sat down with the boys—I still do this occasionally—and I explained to them that our name means something."

"Joseph had just turned three, so he didn't understand," Hailey commented.

Only slightly annoyed, David replied, "Yeah, I know he didn't get it. I still wanted to include him in the conversation, but he gets it more now."

Hailey put up her hands in a defensive posture and smiled. "I'm not arguing. I was just telling them that it was more for Noah at the time."

Everyone giggled at the minor tiff, and David and Hailey laughed it off as well.

"Anyway," David said with emphasis, "my gorgeous, amazing wife and I sat down with the boys and explained that to be in this family means something. We are not here randomly. God created each of us and, through his divine providence, has placed the four of us in this family together. He has a purpose and plan for our lives, and we are to glorify him with the time he gives us."

"You said all of this to a three- and five-year-old?" Brian laughed.

"I know, I know," David acknowledged. "We normally speak very truthfully and practically with them. All that background was simply to make the point with my boys that to be in this family means something. We live a certain way. We act a certain way. We talk a certain way. We treat people a certain way. And we love a certain way. This is *who we are*, and this is what it means to be a Williams."

"David tells them that last part over and over," Hailey explained. "I walked in just the other day as he was standing with Noah next to that picture, sharing those same words with him again. Even though I was only kidding about their young ages, he is right that they are getting it, especially Noah. To be honest, it challenges me personally as well."

Becca slipped her hand up and said, "Can I ask something real quick?"

"Why in the world are you raising your hand, Becca? You can say whatever you want."

Becca and Scott laughed. She shook her head and said, "I don't know what I was thinking, raising my hand. That's embarrassing.

Brian jumped in and said, "Wow, Scott, you must really have her trained well. I can't get my wife to stop talking, and yours raises her hand to speak." Everyone lost it. Becca laughed so hard her face turned red. Moments like these made this group so special. For one hour each week, everyone let their guards down to be their real selves. It was a beautiful thing.

Becca finally asked her question. "In your opinion, what is the real difference between your picture in the hallway and the parenting standard we just finished creating? I know they are not the same, so why do you guys think both are necessary?"

"That's a great question," Hailey responded.

"Yes it is," David agreed. "The answer, in my opinion, is simple. The parenting standard we formed together is a list of fourteen qualities and traits we want to see lived out in our adult children. It is a culmination of the exact kind of young adults we are trying to raise. The list, or standard as I like to call it, simply helps us as parents identify which areas we need to focus on with our children. Then we can intentionally teach and model those characteristics, right?"

"Right," Becca agreed.

David held up his copy of the picture and said, "This is not about the qualities we possess but rather the very essence of who we are and what makes us unique in the eyes of God. This is about our specific family name, and more than that, about the name we wear when we call ourselves Christians. It's about how our family chooses to live and the things that are most important to us. Perhaps most important, it's about creating a true family legacy our children can one day pass down to their children. For us, our family legacy starts with my parents. They were the patriarchs of this information. All I did was to organize it all on paper and add some Scripture. Hailey created that beautiful picture in the hallway."

"I have to admit, I was a bit intimidated when I first started reading that picture," Chris shared, "but now I understand. It's not another list of qualities to instill in our children. It's more of an actual synopsis of who our family is, and the legacy we want to pass on."

"You said it much better than I did," David affirmed with a smile. "Leave it to the smartest guy in the room to wrap things up perfectly tonight."

"Hey, before we finish, I want to read a passage," Hailey insisted. "It's from Psalm seventy-eight. I won't read the whole chapter, but the first part is about exactly what we're talking about tonight: creating and leaving a godly legacy

in our families. We've read this to our kids before, so I have
it highlighted, starting in verse four."

We will not hide God's teaching from their descendants;
we will tell the next generation
the praiseworthy deeds of the Lord,
his power, and the wonders he has done.
He decreed statutes for Jacob
and established the law in Israel,
which he commanded our ancestors
to teach their children,
so the next generation would know them,
even the children yet to be born,
and they in turn would tell their children.
Then they would put their trust in God
and would not forget his deeds
but would keep his commands.

Hailey closed her Bible and added a final thought. "Even
though we fail often, this is the kind of legacy we desire
to create in our family. The reason I asked David to talk
about this, and the reason we are choosing to be real and
vulnerable with what it means to be in the Williams family, is certainly not because anyone else should copy us. It's
because we want to challenge and encourage you guys to
think about your own family legacies. Maybe decide to use
some of what David created, or maybe come up with your
own completely. How you get there doesn't really matter, as
long as you get there."

Everyone was silent. Hailey's powerful words inspired
them. They quietly contemplated their own families. David

looked at his watch. It was already after 7:00 p.m., and they hadn't even gotten to the real stuff yet. "Hailey bet me I couldn't get through this whole thing in one to two weeks, and it looks like she was right. I didn't even get started tonight." He laughed.

"I told you so," Hailey jabbed.

"Oh, well," he said. "I guess we'll tackle it next week."

Brian put his hand on David's shoulder. "Bro, I love you, but do you honestly think we don't expect you to be long-winded?"

CHAPTER SIXTEEN

"Thanks, everyone, for your willingness to meet at our house again this week." Hailey kicked off the small group. "I know it's a longer drive than when we meet at the Clines', so we appreciate it."

"No problem," Brian said. "Your snacks are much better." Everyone laughed at his sarcasm. He was holding a bottle of water and a bowl of mixed fruit, which Hailey had prepared. Jess was known for making incredibly tasty yet extremely unhealthful desserts each week when they met at her home. This was ironic, because she was a personal trainer and quite health-conscious. But for the second week in a row, Hailey had served a more healthful fruit salad. Hailey, not offended by Brian's comment, laughed in agreement. Baking was not her thing.

"Hey, take it easy, Brian," Hailey joked. "I put my heart and soul into cutting up those strawberries."

Leslie patted Brian's belly. "You might want to stick to the fruit for a while, honey."

"Maybe I should as well," David said. Even though Leslie was obviously kidding with her husband, David wanted to take the attention off of Brian, who had gained a few pounds in recent months. He didn't want to see a playful jab turn into a couple's fight, so he purposefully threw himself under the bus and then quickly shifted his attention to the meeting. "Before we pick up where we left off last week, I would love to hear from you guys first. Does anyone have a story to share about what God is doing in your family? Who has begun applying our parenting standard and maybe has a success story? Or have you had any good conversations with your kids this past week?"

The main purpose of this small group was to live life together in true biblical community, and to provide ongoing encouragement and accountability. So the group didn't want to simply create a parenting standard and not take time to discuss it. They had decided they would spend a few minutes each week sharing how God is changing their families. They all agreed to be honest by sharing the good, the bad, and the ugly. Even though they were four separate families, they were acting as one united body of believers with the same goal: to raise their kids to become godly young men and women.

They spent the next fifteen to twenty minutes going around the room and sharing about their kids. They shared personal stories—what was working or not working, good conversations they had with their kids, and offerings of encouragement and advice to one another.

After everyone had a chance to talk, it was time to move into tonight's discussion. "OK, we have about forty-five minutes remaining tonight," David said, "and I have no idea how long this will take or even in what direction it will go. I know I said this last week, but I feel the need to say it again."

"Let me guess—you guys aren't perfect parents, and you don't have it all figured out." Brian said. "We know, and we don't care, buddy."

"I understand, but it's uncomfortable for me to talk about our personal experiences, so I just want to be clear," David replied.

Jess added her two cents by saying, "Brian is right, David. We know you are a humble person, but we all really want to hear more about this. Chris and I haven't stopped talking about our family legacy since last Sunday night. Before now, neither of us had ever thought about, let alone created one for our family. So please, go on."

"Fair enough," David said. "Does everyone have the copy Hailey handed out last week?" All had brought their copies. "We did some introductory stuff last week, so I will just cut to the chase tonight," David said. "Your name means something. To be in your specific family means something very important. I'm not talking only about the broader family of God—I mean you and your specific family. You don't have to answer this now, but think about this question: What kind of legacy are you currently creating and passing down to your children?"

David paused and made eye contact with each person. "Whether we are aware of it or not, we all create a legacy. Sadly, I doubt most families ever take the time to decide exactly what they want their legacy to look like. So instead they go through life randomly, trying their best to be good parents and hoping for a positive outcome. But here is a radical thought: What if you decide ahead of time what it looks like to be a member of your family? What if you choose specifically what your last name really means? And what if your children grow up knowing they belong to something bigger than themselves?"

David held up his copy of the picture from the hallway. "I can summarize this entire thing in two words: *family values.* Hailey and I want to challenge you guys to create your own set of family values." He went around the room and pointed to each couple as he drove home his point. "Scott and Becca, what does it mean to be a Jones? What are the most important values for you and your children to live by? Brian and Leslie, what does it mean to be a Denton? What values and beliefs do you want to pass down to your children and grandchildren? Chris and Jess, what does it mean to be a Cline? What are your nonnegotiables? How do you want your family to be defined? Once you create your own family values, whether you decide to use all of ours, some of ours, or none of ours, I recommend these three steps: 1) display it, 2) discuss it, and 3) live it."

"That's why we have the picture in the hallway," Hailey added. "We have had these family values outlined for almost two years, but we decided several months ago to display it for us all to see on a regular basis, which has been really cool."

"It has made a huge difference, because it's always on our minds now," David agreed. "We walk by it every day, and we refer to it often. Before Hailey made that picture, it was out of sight, out of mind, so we rarely thought about it. The second step is to discuss it."

"I'm sorry to interrupt, but this has been the neatest thing for us," Hailey said. "David and I use this not only as a way to teach the boys, but also in correcting or punishing them."

"Give an example, Hailey," David suggested. "It will make more sense."

"OK, I should share several, but let me see," Hailey thought out loud.

"What about the socks episode a few weeks ago?" David suggested.

"If you have a way to prevent my kids from somehow losing one sock, I'm all ears," Leslie said, smiling.

"No kidding," Chris chimed in. "How is it that socks always go missing? It's one of life's great mysteries."

"Unfortunately I don't have that answer," Hailey responded, "but our kids were notorious for playing outside in only their socks and getting huge holes in the bottoms. A few weeks ago, the boys came in from playing, and you guessed it, they were in socks. Instead of getting mad and yelling, I followed the Lord's more effective approach. I took the boys to the picture in the hallway and told them to read aloud the tenth line. They both said, 'We are wise stewards of the money and resources entrusted to us by God.' Having discussed this before, I asked Noah what it meant to be a steward? He said, 'It's when God let's you be in charge.' I asked the boys what happens when they wear socks outside to play? Joseph looked down like he was ashamed and said, 'They get holes.' It was so cute! I explained that when socks get holes, Mommy has to buy more, which costs extra money. I asked them if they would like me to use money from their piggy banks, and they both said, 'No, ma'am.' And here's the best part for me, because no one wants to be a nagging mom. I said, 'Boys, it means something to be in this family. We are wise stewards of the money and resources God gives us. When you wear your socks outside, you are not only disobeying me, but you are being a poor steward of God's stuff."

"I absolutely adore that story," Becca said. "I love the way you handled it, by making a lasting impression without even yelling or having to punish them."

"Yeah, I agree," Brian added. "No lie, I probably wouldn't have handled myself that well." Brian laughed at his own admission.

David leaned forward and said, "Think about it, guys. The last thing our kids need is another long list of rules to follow. They already have those at home, in school, on sports teams, and even at church. However, there is so much power and long-term impact when we can help our kids connect the decisions they make with the values they profess.

Hailey added, "I'm sure there will come a day when our boys will forget and run outside in their socks. But when it happens, I guarantee they will understand it differently. They won't just see holes in their socks—they will see the unwise stewardship of God's money and resources."

"That's the win!" David exclaimed. "That's when we know we are winning as parents. They will never be perfect, and neither will we. But when everyone in our family is living on purpose and by the same values..." he shook his head, as if realizing the power of his statement. "That's family legacy!"

In typical fashion, Brian spoke up. Only this time, he wasn't trying to be funny or bring attention on himself. Rather, he truly wanted to hear from David and Hailey on the details of their specific family values. Brian really was a good man. Because of his personality and sarcastic humor, he was often misunderstood. But he had come so far in the last two years and changed so much. Since he encountered Christ, he had become a new man, a new husband, a new father, and a new friend. Brian held up his copy of the picture and said, "OK, buddy, let's get to it. I want to hear about this."

David loved Brian's heart, passion, and eagerness to learn. David picked up his copy of the paper and said in an expressive and sarcastic tone, "That leads me to this. If everyone wants to follow along, Brian is ready for us to pick up the pace."

Everyone grabbed their copies, and all the women also sat ready to take notes. The guys were content just following along and listening.

"If it's OK with you guys, I'm going to start from the top and read each of our family values and corresponding Scriptures. I might say a few words about each one, but not much because most are self-explanatory. Honestly, we could spend an entire week discussing each value, but I don't think that's necessary." David looked at Brian and said, "You can hold me accountable. I'm going to be brief and to the point." Brian rolled his eyes to play along. David turned to Hailey and added, "Feel free to jump in with comments so I don't become a talking head."

Without bowing his head or closing his eyes, David said a quick prayer out loud before he began: "Lord, please help me communicate this life-changing information effectively, and may it add value to the lives of my friends and their children."

WHAT DOES IT MEAN TO BE A WILLIAMS?
Our Family Legacy

We live our lives through the lens of Scripture.
All Scripture is God-breathed and is useful for teaching, rebuking, correcting and training in righteousness.
2 Timothy 3:16

"As silly as it might sound," David commented, "Hailey and I tell our kids that if somehow we could take the Bible and embed it into a contact lens and then put that lens in our eyes—*that's* how we should view life...through the lens of Scripture. Just as a contact lens amplifies one's vision, so are we be able to see and understand truth when we look through the lens of Scripture. Likewise we base our beliefs and decisions on Scripture, instead of trying to make Scripture fit our beliefs and decisions. So many people, even churchgoing believers, have it backward. They start with an opinion and then try to distort the truth for their own convenience. That is the very essence of sin. God doesn't ask us to fully understand or comprehend him or his Word, but he does demand our obedience to his Word.

"When an important decision needs to be made, we look to Scripture to help us find the answer. When a controversy arises, we look to Scripture for guidance. When it's time to vote, we vote based on what Scripture teaches. When it's time to meet a spouse, we look to Scripture to find the qualities we desire. The Williamses live their lives by looking through the lens of Scripture."

We value wisdom and discernment above all else.
The beginning of wisdom is this: get wisdom. Though it cost all you have, get understanding. Proverbs 4:7

"I hope no one misunderstands what I am about to say, because we do not minimize the value of a good education. But in our home, we talk more about wisdom and discernment than about knowledge and education. When God told Solomon he could have anything he wanted, Solomon asked for wisdom and discernment. We teach our kids that knowledge can come from a book or class, but wisdom comes only from God.

"We definitely require them to read, study, and learn, but we also teach to pray regularly for God's wisdom. We talk about how valuable discernment is to their personal and professional future. In my humble opinion, the single most important request Christians can make to our heavenly Father is for increased wisdom and discernment. The wiser we become, the better we are in every area of life. The Williamses value wisdom and discernment above all else."

We are sinners saved only by the grace of Jesus Christ.
For it is by grace you have been saved, through faith—and this is not from yourselves, it is the gift of God—not by works, so that no one can boast. Ephesians 2:8–9

"In our culture today, a lie is being taught even in some churches that there are many ways to God and that all roads lead to heaven. Some even teach that we can earn our way to heaven by living a good life, going to church, or doing good deeds for humanity. We, however, teach our children the truth. We tell them there is absolutely nothing we can do to earn the love of Christ and forgiveness of God. We will never be good enough, but Jesus is.

"The greatest realization our children can come to is that they are sinners in need of a Savior. As parents we can tell them this truth until we are blue in the face, but it isn't until they discover it personally that they can be saved. Our legacy has no value if it doesn't include the salvation of every member of our family. The Williamses believe we are sinners saved only by the grace of Jesus Christ."

We love and support other members of our family.
Anyone who does not provide for their relatives, and especially for their own household, has denied the faith and is worse than an unbeliever. 1 Timothy 5:8

"I tell the boys often, 'Mommy and I will always love you unconditionally, but you will also always respect us completely.' Nothing is stronger than the bond of family, but nothing can be more damaging than breaking that bond. We must protect this bond, starting with the man, the head of the household. I must honor my wife and remain faithful to her. By doing that, I earn her respect. And my wife remains submissive and supportive of my leadership. By doing that, she earns my love.

"Our family is not going to agree on everything, but other than our eternal relationship with Jesus, nothing or no one is more important than the relationship we have with one another. We might argue from time to time, but we always have one another's backs. We are best friends for life. Friends come and go, but family sticks together forever.

For that reason, we don't ask our children to just coexist together. Instead, we encourage them to be the closest of friends. The Williamses love and support other members of our family."

We are great leaders when it's time to lead and great followers when we need to follow.
Jesus called them together and said, "You know that those who are regarded as rulers of the Gentiles lord it over them, and their high officials exercise authority over them. Not so with you. Instead, whoever wants to become great among you must be your servant, and whoever wants to be first must be slave of all. For even the Son of Man did not come to be served, but to serve, and to give his life as a ransom for many." Mark 10:42–45

"Our boys are too young to fully understand leadership, but they are never too young to learn and apply certain leadership principles. One principle that Hailey and I teach them often is that leadership is not about a position or title, nor is it about telling people what to do. True biblical leadership is about positively influencing people, adding value to their lives, and serving the masses.

"Again, the buck stops here with me. It is my God-given duty to lead my family by example. I am commanded to lead them spiritually and to set the moral tone for our family. Another biblical truth we are trying to instill is that, as Christians, we are all leaders *and* followers. I believe we should constantly be leading and following at the same time. To be an effective leader, I must also follow someone else who teaches and inspires. And at the same time, even followers are leading others to where they are in life.

"Jesus led by serving the masses. He is our greatest example and inspiration. We tell our boys to always be on the lookout for opportunities to serve. When you see a need, don't wait to be asked—get in there and do it. To influence and impact others in school, sports, work, church, or wherever, we must learn how to be servant leaders. The Williamses are great leaders when it's time to lead and great followers when we need to follow."

We treat all people with dignity and respect.
Do nothing out of selfish ambition or vain conceit. Rather, in humility value others above yourselves. Philippians 2:3

"Noah is only six, but I bet I started telling him this when he was only three or four. I say, 'You are no better than anyone else, buddy, but guess what—no one else is better than you either.' If there's anything I love in life, it's when a person knows God values everyone equally. That is the epitome of the gospel. Hailey feels the same."

David looked at Hailey and asked if she wanted to comment, but she didn't. Although she had strong feelings about this and other values, she knew he was in his zone and wanted him to continue uninterrupted.

"There will always be certain people we like better or enjoy being around more. And likewise, there will always be certain people we don't hang out with because of their behavior or lifestyle. But the reason Hailey and I included this as a core family value is because we want our boys to realize God creates everyone in his image and loves us all equally.

Regardless of a person's job, income level, race, gender, religion, or background, we should treat everyone with the dignity and respect they deserve.

"However, I do make sure my boys know this doesn't mean we should associate with just anyone. We are known by the company we keep and should surround ourselves only with like-minded people who challenge and encourage us to become better. Like attracts like. You can love a person but choose to not be his or her friend, or you can respectfully disagree with another person's lifestyle or choices without ruining your witness with him or her. The Williamses try to treat all people with dignity and respect."

Before David could move on to the next family value, Hailey motioned to her watch that it was getting late. "Do we want to try to finish next Sunday?" she asked.

"I'm so sorry," David replied, somewhat embarrassed. "I had no idea how late it was. You guys know I can get going sometimes."

Still writing as fast as she could in her notebook, Jess shook her head and said, without looking up, "Don't apologize. This has been so meaningful for me tonight." She finally put her pen down and rubbed her hands.

Leslie laughed. "Are your hands hurting as bad as mine?" she asked. "I haven't taken this many notes since college."

Brian looked over at his wife's notebook, which was full of scribbled notations. "I didn't even take that many notes in college," he joked.

Scott hadn't taken notes but was laser-focused on everything David said. Scott was a great husband and father, so what he said next made a great impact on David. "That was probably the best parental advice I've ever received, David. Becca and I have been to three different Christian parenting or family conferences over the years, and that was more beneficial than anything I have learned. I'm excited to hear more about these family values next week. I know Becca and I will discuss how to create and share our own family legacy."

Scott's comment almost brought David to tears. He wasn't normally an emotional man, but for some reason the topic of parenting brought out his most sensitive side. He nodded for a few seconds, giving him time to swallow the lump in his throat. Finally under control, he replied, "Thank you so much for your kind words, Scott. Coming from you, that is a true compliment."

Hailey took a playful jab at her husband, adding, "I told you everyone would enjoy hearing about this. Lesson learned: always listen to your wife."

"Amen!" Jess shouted. "I can't think of a more perfect way to end tonight."

David agreed. "I hope everyone has a blessed week. I think we can finish this up next Sunday, if we start on time and jump right into it."

"Did you hear that, honey?" Brian asked his wife. "That means no long-winded stories about who got voted off of some reality TV show or who posted what on Facebook."

CHAPTER SEVENTEEN

WHAT DOES IT MEAN TO BE A WILLIAMS?
(continued)

We speak with words of honesty, wisdom, love, and encouragement.
Do not let any unwholesome talk come out of your mouths, but only what is helpful for building others up according to their needs, that it may benefit those who listen. Ephesians 4:29

"The words we choose—or avoid—say so much about who we are as people," David began at the next small group meeting. "Our words matter. One of the greatest lies our culture has ever produced is the idea that 'sticks and stones may break my bones, but words will never hurt me.' This is a bold-faced lie. We teach our boys that our words have the ability to speak life into people as well as the potential to destroy them. I ask them, 'Boys, would you rather build people up or tear them down? You have the power to do both, and that's a huge responsibility.'

"Hailey and I deeply desire to be known as a family who speaks truth and encourages others. Anytime our boys get punished, we remind them that the worst thing they can do is lie to us. Lying is more offensive to us than whatever it is they might be trying to cover up. God honors and blesses those who speak truth in love.

"Once again, it starts with me. I don't always succeed, but I make a conscious effort to compliment Hailey in front of the kids. I want them to hear me say nice things to their mother. Hailey is the best I've ever seen at giving positive feedback and encouragement to our boys. I don't mean coddling them or telling them constantly how great they are—that can be counterproductive in the long-term. But she is very intentional about looking for the things they do right or well and then praising them for it. I have a tendency to be too critical, because my expectations of my kids are so high. I have definitely learned from my wife on this one. We desire to create a legacy of speaking with words of honesty, wisdom, love and encouragement."

We learn how to think differently, for our thoughts create our lives.

Finally, brothers and sisters, whatever is true, whatever is noble, whatever is right, whatever is pure, whatever is lovely, whatever is admirable—if anything is excellent or praiseworthy— think about such things. Philippians 4:8

"I could talk about this for hours," David pointed to Brian and added, "but I won't. I have been studying and reading about this topic for several years, so it's very important to me. I have always believed our choices determine where we end up in life, and to a degree it's true. But what creates our choices? What I have learned is that our thoughts create our choices, which determine our future. It all starts with the way we think. I encourage you to read any book by Andy Andrews, Jack Canfield, Jim Rohn, or Napoleon Hill.

"This is easier said than done, but as parents we must help our children learn *how* to think, not just *what* to think. School teaches them what to think, but there is so much more to life, especially when they enter the real world. I teach the boys this awesome quote from Albert Einstein: 'A problem cannot be solved by the same consciousness that created it.' Parents can be really good at solving their kids' problems, but shouldn't we instead help them learn to solve their own problems? From my experience, the best way I've found to accomplish this is by asking good questions. I teach my kids to ask questions that force their minds to go to work on how to solve a problem or issue.

"Here's a quick example from what we did with Noah several weeks ago. He really wanted to buy a video game, but he didn't have enough money saved. Instead of saying, 'Here's some extra money,' or, 'Oh, well, it's too expensive,' I said to him, 'If you really want this game, think about how you can buy it. Put your mind to work, and come up with some options of how you can earn enough money to buy it soon.' It's a silly example, but instead of just saying it cost too much—that's the *what*—I encouraged him to think about a solution—that's the *how*.

"Instilling this value first in ourselves and then in our children takes many years, so start now. Get a book or two from one of the authors I mentioned, and retrain your brain on how to think more positively. Our thoughts create our lives. Wherever we are in life and whatever circumstances we face, we created it with our thoughts. The Williamses learn how to think differently, for our thoughts create our lives."

We live not only for this life but also for eternity.
What good is it for someone to gain the whole world, yet forfeit their soul? Mark 8:36

"We have not yet taught this value to our boys, simply because of their ages, but it will be a top priority as they get older and develop their own personal relationships with Jesus. When I was in high school, my dad encouraged me to intentionally build friendships with kids for the purpose of sharing my faith with them. He called it relational evangelism, and it's the same strategy I have used since I was a teenager, and I teach it to my students. Hailey is even better at this than I am, but we both always try to have at least one person in our lives to build a relationship with, praying for an opportunity to hopefully lead them to Christ.

"Depending on which statistics you read, somewhere between sixty and seventy percent of Christians will never lead another person to Christ—not one! I believe relational evangelism is the most effective and rewarding way to share the love of Jesus. Our goal is to make this a priority for Noah and Joseph. They don't need to become Bible scholars or ministers, unless God calls them of course. But we desire them to have a heart for sharing Christ with others. We hope to pass down a legacy of intentionally building relationships with unbelievers—or 'loving people to Jesus's as my father used to say. In other words, we want part of our family legacy to include living not only for this life, but for eternity to come."

We are wise stewards of the money and resources entrusted to us by God.
The wise store up choice food and olive oil, but fools gulp theirs down. Proverbs 21:20

"Did any of you attend the Dave Ramsey financial class I taught a couple of years ago? That was before we started this group, so I don't remember if you were there." Everyone shook his or her head no. "I highly recommend you take that class next time it's offered. Dave Ramsey is the man, and his wisdom is life-changing if you apply it. Of course, Chris knows this stuff way more than me. Anyway, one thing I said every week in that class is that money is not the most important thing in life, but practically speaking, teaching our children about money will do more good and prevent more harm than almost any other lesson. It must be a pretty significant matter to God, because he talks as much in the Bible about money, finances, and stewardship as almost anything else.

"Hailey and I talk openly and honestly about money in our home. We purposefully teach our boys money lessons, beginning when they were four years old. Let me be very clear that, while there is nothing wrong with a person earning a crazy amount of wealth, I'm not talking about getting rich. What the Bible teaches—what we want our children to learn and practice—is that God instructs us to be wise with the money and resources he freely gives. Part of that wisdom includes teaching our boys how to handle money, how to save, how to invest, how to negotiate, how to avoid debt, how to make wise purchases, how to tithe, how to bless others, and how to take proper care of our possessions.

"We don't have to be as smart of Chris when it comes to investing, but I do believe all Christian parents have the responsibility to raise their kids with a biblical understanding of money. Remember, guys, we're talking about building a legacy that's passed down for generations. How cool would it be if our children and grandchildren were to avoid all the money mistakes we have made? The Williamses want to be wise stewards of the money and resources entrusted to us by God."

We never blame others but rather own our decisions, including successes and failures.
So then, each of us will give an account of ourselves to God. Romans 14:12

"When I was growing up, we were not allowed to say, 'That's not fair.' My parents called it *the forbidden phrase.* They taught me that life doesn't always seem fair but that the worst thing I can do is make excuses and blame others. This life lesson has stuck with me ever since, and now we teach it to our boys. Blaming others is an instinct that lives within us, starting at a young age. Because it's an inclination, it must therefore be released and replaced. It's very much connected to the principle of changing the way we think, which we discussed earlier.

"The biggest problem in blaming others for our situations in life is that it removes personal responsibility. It's way easier to point fingers at someone or something else than it is to accept responsibility. I've said this before to you guys, and I'm sure I'll say it again, but here is one of the most hardcore truths I have learned in life: *I am who I am, I am where I am, and I have what I have in life because of my own choices...period.* Some people might say this is harsh, but that's not how our family chooses to live.

"I tell the boys it's *never* the boss's fault or the economy's fault or the spouse's fault or the government's fault or the weather's fault or the pharmaceutical industry's fault or the doctor's fault or a coworker's fault or the teacher's fault or the coach's fault...and the list goes on and on. When we take ownership of our decisions, we transition from good to great in life. This is true in every area of our lives.

"Guys, this isn't theory—this has been true and relevant in our family. Our marriage struggled for years, until we stopped blaming each other for every problem and worked on improving ourselves as individuals. Our finances struggled for years until we stopped overspending and going into debt and learned to better manage our money. Our health struggled for years until we stopped eating and drinking junk all the time and instead ate healthy and worked out. Hailey and I took ownership of our lives and our family. We still have struggles and issues, no doubt. But when they arise, instead of blaming someone else, we take personal responsibility. That's the legacy we hope to pass on to our boys. The Williamses never blame others; rather, we own our decisions, including our success and failures."

We choose to be grateful and thankful in all circumstances.
Give thanks in all circumstances; for this is God's will for you in Christ Jesus. 1 Thessalonians 5:18

"My father taught me many great truths before he died, but one of the most beneficial was to always be thankful. We had a bench in our front yard that he called *the thankful bench*. We sat on the bench every once in a while and talked back and forth about all we were thankful for. When I was young, I thought it was the coolest thing ever. As a teenager, I felt like it was silly and juvenile, but he made me do it anyway. Now Hailey and I do this with our kids.

"I desperately want our boys to be grateful and thankful for the Lord's many blessings. Many of you have been around us enough to know how important this value is to our family. We constantly remind the boys how blessed we are, and we are very intentional about helping them to be grateful. Remember, our flesh is selfish by nature, so we have to persistently instill gratitude. Anytime we do something fun as a family, we always end with everyone sharing a few things we are thankful for.

"I know this might sound remedial, but I believe that so few parents are purposeful about teaching gratitude. And honestly, I don't even think it's intentional. It's just much easier for us to focus on what we don't have or things that aren't going well. This should be a reminder to all parents that our kids listen to our conversations. Are they hearing us constantly complain and then in the next sentence tell them to be grateful? What kind of examples do we set? The good news is that gratitude is a choice. In our Christian families, we either choose each day to be thankful or allow the events of each day to determine our attitude. We have struggles and bad days, but we are focused on improving in this area. The Williamses choose to be grateful and thankful in all circumstances."

We value our health—God only gives us one body, so we honor it.

Do you not know that your bodies are temples of the Holy Spirit, who is in you, whom you have received from God? You are not your own; you were bought at a price. Therefore honor God with your bodies. 1 Corinthians 6:19–20

"I think we all agree so much pressure is put on teenagers and young adults today to look a certain way. I see it daily in my job, especially when I spend time on school campuses. But this value we want to pass down to our children has nothing to do with size, weight, or stylish clothes. Hailey and I are both passionate about being healthy, and we want our children to be as well. Let me ask you guys a rhetorical question: Don't you believe that God desires for his children to live in perfect health and well-being?

"Neither one of us are fitness gurus or nutritionists, but we try to apply some common sense in our home. We like to use the phrase *health consciousness* in our family. We want the boys to be conscious and aware of the choices they make when it comes to food, exercise, and medication. Like Scripture says, are we honoring our bodies? Far too many people *choose* to eat poorly each day, neglect exercise for years, and depend on medication, and then when they are utterly sick and unhealthy, they blame someone else. 'The doctors can't heal me; the medications make me feel worse; my weight is hereditary; I'm too tired to exercise; I'm addicted to food...'

"The bottom line is this: we choose to either be healthy or take what comes our way. Either way, we decide. We are in charge of our own bodies. We are not victims. How much of a priority is our health? I ask this question because if we treat our bodies wisely, then our kids will probably follow suit. I encourage you to talk about health consciousness in your families. Discuss wise food choices. Splurge occasionally, but make it the exception and not the rule. Inspire your kids to exercise and run around. And finally, use medication as a last resort, not a first response. This is one of Hailey's biggest passions, but we better not get her going or we will be here all night. She taught me that medication might treat a system, but only eating healthfully can prevent or solve the problem. The Williamses choose to be healthy and to honor God with our bodies."

We are guided by values, morals, and principles, not by the changing culture.
But if serving the Lord seems undesirable to you, then choose for yourselves this day whom you will serve, whether the gods your ancestors served beyond the Euphrates, or the gods of the Amorites, in whose land you are living. But as for me and my household, we will serve the Lord. Joshua 24:15

"Often I speak to students who genuinely love Jesus, but they struggle with the relevancy of Scripture. They say things like, 'I know the Bible says such and such, but times are different now,' or, 'So many things have changed,' or 'Most people don't believe that anymore,' or, 'It's old and dated.' My response to them is always consistent, and it's the same thing we will pass on to our boys. Absolute truth doesn't change with the culture. Far too many people, and even some believers, try so hard to change Scripture in order to fit their beliefs and lifestyles. Hailey and I teach our boys the exact opposite. As Christians, we surrender to Christ and to the Word of God.

"Cultural beliefs and practices constantly change. What is acceptable and celebrated in society is different from year to year and country to country. Basing beliefs, morals, and principles on an ever-changing culture undermines the inerrancy of Scripture. We teach our kids that God does not change, and the Bible does not change. We have to decide once and for all if we are going to follow culture or Christ. In my household we choose to serve the Lord. We are sinners and certainly get many things wrong, but there is one thing Hailey and I both know to be true: the Williamses are guided by biblical values, morals, and principles, not by the changing culture."

We are quick to forgive others, because Jesus is quick to forgive us.
Bear with each other and forgive one another if any of you has a grievance against someone. Forgive as the Lord forgave you. Colossians 3:13

"I will be brief, because it should go without saying that forgiveness is at the foundation of Christian life. But as it relates to parenting and our family legacy, Hailey and I desire to create an atmosphere of grace and mercy. We talk a lot with our boys about forgiveness. When they do something wrong or have a bad attitude, we encourage them to not only apologize to whomever they offended but also to ask for forgiveness. I believe, because I have witnessed it many times in ministry, that one of the most dangerous things a Christian can do is hold onto anger, resentment, and bitterness for long periods of time. It can literally manifest into physical ailments and emotional issues.

"My advice to all parents is to lay the foundation in your family of what it looks like to extend forgiveness, grace, and mercy to those we feel have offended us. We must, of course, have rules, and there should be punishment for breaking those rules. Scripture is very clear about how dangerous and unwise it is to let a child go without discipline. But here is where we can win as parents: we should never leave our children in their sin. In other words, after the punishment is given, then we are responsible for restoring our child back into good graces. We do this with forgiveness. As parents, we lead the way by asking our children to forgive us when we mess up or go too far. Set the example, Mom and Dad. Ultimately everything goes back to Jesus. Therefore, the Williamses are quick to forgive others because Jesus is quick to forgive us."

We use our gifts and talents to glorify God and serve others.
Each of you should use whatever gift you have received to serve others, as faithful stewards of God's grace in its various forms. 1 Peter 4:10

"Although this is our final family value, it is not the least important. I believe with all my heart that God creates every person with a unique set of abilities and talents, all of which are valuable to him. If God knits us together with a specific giftedness, how selfish would we be to not use it for his glory? The coolest truth is that all gifts and talents are equally beneficial to the kingdom.

"My advice to parents is to help your children discover their God-given abilities and then encourage them to use those gifts to serve the church and others. As Christian adults, we lead the way and set the example. So I offer you, my friends, some questions to think about. What are your God-given gifts? What talents and abilities do you have that many others don't? What life experiences do you have that, if shared, could help someone else? What specifically are you doing right now to serve your church? How do you use your gifts to help and serve others?

"How cool would it be if we cared as much about our children's spiritual gifts as we do their academics and athletics? Sure, we want our kids to excel in school and sports, but it's not everything for us. Wouldn't their lives be incomplete if they got straight As and were starters on every sports team but never used their gifts to help others? Would God be satisfied with us as parents or them as his children? I'm not sure. But I am sure of this: the Williams family may not be great at much, but we use whatever gifts and abilities God has given us for his glory."

David sat back in his chair, contemplating whether or not he was finished sharing. He had been talking for over an hour, but it felt like only minutes had passed. He was having so much fun. Teaching was his gift, and adding real value to families was his passion. David was loving every second of it.

"I want to make one last comment," he said as he straightened up. "I heard a fantastic quote once from one of my favorite authors, Andy Andrews. If you don't follow his podcast, *In The Loop*, you really should. Andy said, 'Do not allow what everyone perceives as normal to be your guide.' When it comes to biblical parenting, I can't think of better advice for us to close on. Let's be honest, guys, this stuff is challenging." David held up the notes he had been speaking from. "It's way easier to be an average parent than an excellent parent. It's way easier to raise great kids than it is to raise great young adults."

David again waved his notes over his head. "Parenting this way isn't normal, but you and I are not guided by crowds or culture or by what's normal or easy. We are guided by the truth of Scripture and the wisdom of the Holy Spirit in our lives. Because of that, we are purposeful and intentional about raising our children according to God's Word. We will create and pass down a family legacy that inspires others. No matter how long it takes or how difficult it is, that is our mission and calling."

Hailey cleared her throat. "May I say something, honey?"

"Of course...please," he answered. "I've been talking so long that even I am tired of listening to myself."

"It's wonderful, honey. I love what you just said about us not wanting to be normal. I've never thought about parenting that way, but why on earth would any of us want to be normal or raise our children like the world does?" A few made affirming comments. Hailey continued, "There's nothing I can add to what my husband has said, guys, but I'd like to conclude this way. If any of this sounds over-whelming, I totally relate. It overwhelms me, even after two years of living this way. Although it might seem overwhelm-ing in this moment, remember that this is not an overnight change. We have a lifetime to create and pass down our family legacies to our children. There is no certain time frame with this. Another thing I want to say is that we have not fully accomplished all these family values David has been sharing. And I promise we haven't perfected *any* of them. Some we've barely spent much time on yet because of the young ages of the boys."

"That's so true," David said.

"I wanted David to teach on this is because I know you guys care about your children just as much as we do ours." Hailey got choked up. "You guys all care just as much about your family legacy as we do ours." She gathered herself. "It doesn't matter if you decide to use all of, some of, or none of the values we hold most dear. What is important is that we all understand that we can create whatever legacies we want for our families. It wasn't until two years ago that David and I sat down together and wrote out these specific values, which are most important to us. Up until then, we had never even thought about it before." Hailey grabbed David by the hand and gave him a cute smile. "Thank you for taking the lead on this," she said. David returned the smile and squeezed her hand tightly.

Hailey turned her attention back to the group. "I want to encourage you to sit down together and create your own family values. Don't rush it, but don't put it off either. Make it a priority, and get it down together. Have fun with it—after all, it's your family. When you are finished, go to work on improving yourselves in each of those areas. Teach your children what these values mean and why they are important to you. And here's the best part," Hailey concluded. "Lord willing, our kids will eventually share these same values with their children."

"Legacy!" David said. "A godly legacy."

CHAPTER EIGHTEEN

Everyone from small group had gone home, and the Williams family was starting its bedtime routine. Nighttime was always very special for David and Hailey. Even when they were exhausted from a long and busy day, they made it a priority to give the boys their very best at night, instead of just giving them what was left. But like everyone else, they had bad days from time to time. They had learned to lean on each other for help when those days came. They didn't want to simply send their kids to bed. They desired to be with them during the final minutes of each day. So whenever one parent was exhausted or sick, the other picked up the slack.

Sunday night was a particularly special time in the Williamses' home. Each week on Sunday night, they started their bedtime routine about fifteen minutes early so they would have time for a weekly family devotion. Although they read from the book of Proverbs each morning before school, prayed together daily as a family, and attended church twice a week, this was a uniquely special time for them all. They weren't rushed, and they didn't have anywhere to be or anything more important to do.

They read from a devotional book with Scripture, or sometimes they read a story from the Bible. David usually did the reading, but sometimes he asked one of the boys to read instead. Afterward they spent a few minutes discussing what they had just read. Hailey usually asked the boys a couple of questions about the devotional thought or Bible passage. The goal was simply to get the boys talking and discussing God's Word. David and Hailey didn't just recite content—they tried to make it a family discussion. Some nights the boys fired back with a few questions of their own: What does that verse mean? I don't understand—why would God do that? Why do you think Jesus said that?

David's favorite thing to do was engage them with open-ended questions designed not for them to respond with a memorized answer but to get them thinking. He used what he called *situational questions*, which were intended to get the boys prepared for real-life situations they might face one day. David's philosophy was that instead of avoiding the topic, prepare them for the day they'd face the situation. He frequently asked questions such as these: If you were in this situation, how do you think you would handle it? If your schoolteacher ever said this, how would you respond? If you were at a place and this happened, how would you get out of it? If you had a friend who did this, what would your reaction be?

After their devotional, Scripture reading, and discussion, they quickly read through their family values. Depending on what happened during the week, or maybe if one of the boys struggled in a specific area, David might choose to highlight a particular value to discuss its importance in detail. Otherwise, they just skimmed through the list each week with a different family member doing the reading.

They ended each Sunday night with a family prayer that was usually longer than how they typically prayed together other nights of the week at bedtime. They discussed any issues, problems, needs, or praises that were relevant that week. Then each person decided which needs they wanted to pray for. The cutest times were when the boys argued over who got to pray for a certain person. They sat in a circle, holding hands, as they took turns praying out loud for each issue or person. When finished, each one would squeeze the hand of the next person to pray. When everyone had prayed, David always closed the prayer by thanking God for his many blessings and asking for his hedge of protection around his family.

After the family devotional, the boys went to their rooms. David and Hailey then tuck them each into bed separately. During this time David did what he called "check their hearts." He learned it while attending a conference led by his favorite speaker and author, Andy Andrews. Andy shared with the audience how he ends each day with his own kids. David loved it so much that he began doing it immediately and had continued each night ever since. Even when David was out of town, Hailey contacted him through FaceTime so he could chat with the boys and "check their hearts" at bedtime.

The exercise was the exact same for both sons, but he started with Noah, his older. With the lights out and Noah under the covers, David placed his right hand over Noah's heart. "It's time to check your heart, buddy. Let me feel this thing and make sure it's working right." David rubbed Noah's chest. "Do you know how much I love you, buddy?"

"Yes, sir," Noah replied.

"Do you know how much your mother and brother love you?"

"Yes, sir."

"And do you know how much God loves you?"

"Yes, sir, I do."

"Are you proud of yourself today? Are you proud of how you behaved?"

"Yes, I am."

"Is there anything you did today that you wish you had done differently—maybe something no one knows about? The Bible tells us to confess our sins, and he will forgive us. Is there anything we need to ask God to forgive you for?" David asked.

"No, sir, not today."

"Is there anyone you are upset with—anyone who did something bad or mean to you today? The Bible says not to go to bed angry, so is there anyone you need to forgive tonight?"

"No, sir, it was a good day," Noah answered.

David patted his six-year-old son on the chest and said, "Sleep well, buddy, because you have a great heart. Tomorrow is going to be a wonderful day." David kissed his son on the cheek and asked, "Is there anything else you want to talk about?"

"No, sir, nothing important tonight," Noah said.

"Good night, Noah."

"Good night, Daddy."

David walked out and turned into Joseph's room. He knelt next to the bed and placed his hand on his four-year-old son's heart.

Also available from Jamie Dewald...

HIS FINAL
GIFT

25 Lessons for Fathers

JAMIE DEWALD

Made in the USA
Charleston, SC
24 February 2017